IRONSIDE

HEARTBREAKER MC #3

ALEXIS ABBOTT

PATHFORGERS PUBLISHING

Get an EXCLUSIVE book, **FREE** just as a thank you for signing up for my newsletter! Plus you'll never miss a new release, cover reveal, or promotion!

http://alexisabbott.com/newsletter

READING ORDER:

Don't miss out on the rest of the Heartbreakers Series by Alexis Abbott!

Breaker
Bones
Ironside
Big Daddy

IRONSIDE

*H*ot black coffee runs down my throat as my eyes watch the pink glow of the neon sign that barely stands out above the new strip club in the fading sunset light. From the diner across the street, I'm watching the place before it opens for the evening.

Diesel is here. I know he is.

It's been a long time since I had the kind of company you get at a strip club, but this is a different kind of joint. There have been rumors about shit I don't like to see in my state surrounding this place, and it turned up out of nowhere almost overnight. That tells me something's up, and it reeks of Diesel, the biker whose gang has been pimping out women against their will at clubs like this all over the state.

That doesn't seem to bother the patrons, though.

Pickings are slim in this one-stoplight Wyoming town off the interstate, so last night, the parking lot was packed with trucks...and motorcycles.

I parked my own bike a few buildings down, out of sight. I don't want anyone in that strip club knowing I'm here until I'm good and ready to show myself. Because as soon as someone in that club gets eyes on me, shit's going to turn hot real fast. That's not how I operate. I'm quick, I'm quiet, and when I strike I do *not* miss.

If I weren't I wouldn't be alive right now.

As long as I'm in the back of this diner, I can take my time. I look like anyone else from across the street. My black boots are dusty, my blue jeans are tattered, and my old dog tags rest on my military-green shirt. They're the same ones I wore in the Marines, but they don't look like they did back then. I had them melted down and re-stamped to show that I'm Ironside, and I'm a Heartbreaker.

As if my kutte couldn't do that on its own, that is. The tattered Heartbeaker colors rest on my shoulders, all but falling apart except for the pristine patches, some of which have been with me since my military days.

Wearing those colors around here means something. This is not our territory, but it's close enough to it that people know what the Heartbreaker emblem means. The skeletal hands spearing a heart have the respect of the locals on this side of the state.

They know we keep the peace. We don't let predators rule these roads. We keep them clean.

And cleaning up is what I'm here to do.

The club's front doors swing open, and I see two men file out, squinting to keep the sunlight out of their eyes from that direction. I make note of that. They're bikers, that much is obvious even from across the street. They're not wearing their kuttes, but the rest of the look is a dead giveaway.

And I recognize one of them.

The shorter one of the two is a guy with a slight limp that makes his gait easy to recognize. When I knew him, he was a prospect back in Buzz's MC. When the Heartbreakers put Buzz six feet under the dry earth, we hoped his sex slavery ring would go down with it. We were wrong. Diesel was one of his right-hand men, and people rallied around him in the name of making money. This guy must have stuck around Diesel and just put on new colors.

I've had a gut feeling this is either Diesel's new stronghold or one of them, but I need proof. Breaker, our leader, won't make a move against a club like this unless we know for damn sure there's shady business going on behind its doors. And that means I need to get on the other side of them.

The two guys head around the building and disappear behind a corner, chatting to each other as they go. I'm not going to be able to see much more from here. But I've watched a van go behind that building, and there's been no more activity since those two went back there. That tells me it's a good place to start.

I leave the cash for my tab and a fat tip on the table before heading for the door, taking out a pair of aviators and putting them on. My boots crunch across the asphalt as I casually make my way to the curb and cross the empty street, glancing over my shoulder and keeping my stride confident.

The sun is in the eyes of anyone who comes out of the club or sticks their head out, there are no windows in the front, and I look like I belong there at a glance. In a few hours, they'll have sentries out prowling on the rooftops, but for now, it's business as usual upstairs. The only people milling around are bikers, some of them probably prospects who might not even recognize my face.

Breaking into a place in broad daylight isn't always that hard. Sometimes, walking with a stride that tells people you belong here and are on your way to something is all you need to be convincing. Since gunshots don't start firing the second I step into the club parking lot, I figure luck is on my side.

I cased the building this morning. The two guys I saw must be heading around to the back side of the building, which could mean they're checking on the AC unit, but more likely means they're heading around to the back of the building, where there's an exit from the club's basement. It also means I've only got so much time to follow them and stay out of earshot.

When I reach the corner of the club, I see the two of them disappear behind the back corner, presumably heading for the basement. I keep low and follow them, thinking. The only reason they'd need to go to the basement would be to unlock the doors for the night, in case someone needs to get in or out in a hurry. That means one of them probably has his keys out.

Sure enough, by the time I'm close enough to the AC unit to crouch low behind it, I hear the sound of jingling keys coming my way. I press myself against the unit and wait as I hear the two men approach. They're not chatting anymore, and that's a problem. Conversation keeps people distracted and easy to pickpocket.

I wait and hold my breath, and when the men stride past the AC unit, I reach out.

Moments later, I watch them disappear behind the front corner of the strip club again while I clutch the keys between my fingers and slip around back.

When I approach, I'm surprised to see the basement doors locked up with a padlock and heavy chain. So, they weren't back here unlocking it, meaning they probably want this door locked all night when the bar opens.

I'm not surprised.

That means they have something down there they want to keep *in*.

After one more glance around the back of the building, I crouch down and open the padlock as quietly as I can, and I slide the chains aside. I shouldn't be doing this alone, but if Diesel is working out of this place, a lone man like me is able to get in and out better than a crew of us would.

I pull the door open with one hand, and I hold the huge, heavy steel padlock in my other. It's coming with me. Fading light floods the stairs as I slip in and shut the door behind me without so much as a glance over my shoulder. Just like that, I'm on a mission again, and my training kicks in.

My steps are completely silent as I slip into the shadows of the club's basement. It leads to a larger room that opens up at the base of the stairs, and I carefully take out a hand mirror I brought to check around the corner.

A stone falls to my stomach.

It looks like an average club basement at a glance--shelves of scant supplies line the walls, and there's a man leaning by the entrance to what looks like a janitor's closet.

Guards aren't usually posted on janitor's closets, and I think my suspicions about what that lock was for are about to be confirmed. But I don't want to make noise and let the guard call in a dozen more men in on me. I glance around me, mind racing.

I notice a tall plastic bucket sitting by the door, and after taking a deep, silent breath, I kick it over. I hear a grunt from the guard, who approaches carefully, eyes down as if looking for an animal who'd slipped inside. Before he even sees me, I move.

My fist lashes out, and the steel padlock cracks him across the head. He staggers and looks up at me with hazy eyes before toppling over to the ground. I clutch the padlock and check the man's pulse to make sure he's alive before moving on to the closet.

My face pales at what I see within.

Instead of any equipment, there's a thick, scratchy blanket bundled up on a wet concrete floor in a tight roll...and there's a shock of strawberry blonde hair spilling out of one end of it. Quickly, I stoop down and put my hands on the woman's shoulders, and I'm relieved to at least feel warmth.

There might be hope.

I pull back the blankets carefully, and I find that they've been wrapped tight around her. Her body is limp, and I start worrying that I might be too late before I find a wrist and put my fingers to it.

She has a pulse. She must be drugged.

I pull the blankets down from her face, and I'm nearly stunned by the sight. She has the face of an angel, like a marble statue brought to life--and about as pale to match, too.

Clutching the girl in my arms, I curse silently. She can't be a day over twenty, and she must have been taken recently. She looks like a healthy person, despite her condition right now. I wonder how recently she ended up here, and how, but I don't have time for that. It's only a matter of minutes before someone else has reason to come down here, or the man I just knocked out gets missed.

I've got to make a call on what to do, immediately.

This is Diesel's place, this is all the proof I need of that. The smart thing to do would be to just snap pictures of what I've seen, send them to Breaker, and organize a raid. But that could put her life in more danger, and as if that weren't enough, it would leave her to face whatever they have planned for her tonight.

And this is Diesel's gang. What he has planned isn't going to be pretty. Anger boils my blood, and for a moment, I let myself start to plan heading upstairs and taking them all on, armed with nothing but my padlock. I'd faced worse odds before and pulled out on top. But I've got to get this girl out of harm, and there's only one surefire way to do that.

I've got to steal her.

"Hey," I whisper to her, brushing her hair away from her ear. "Can you hear me? I'm a friend. Talk to me, honey."

Her head rolls limp to the side, and I scoop her into my arms and pick her up. I know what I'm going to do. I knew as soon as I saw her, truth be told, but my better judgment still rears its head every now and then.

I carry her up the stairs, moving as silently as I did on the way up here. I've carried bodies far bulkier than hers before in worse conditions. The weight on my mind is much heavier, anyway. Stealing this girl from Diesel isn't just deadly in the short term. There will be consequences.

"Alright, girl," I murmur to her softly as I carry her. "If I get you out of here, you're gonna need to hold on tight, and keep your head down. It's a long way to the clubhouse."

The sounds of my boots on the ground and my husky breathing are all I can focus on as my legs carry me across the second asphalt driveway behind another abandoned business near the club. With the girl in my arms, stealth is all but out of the question. I've got to make a break for it and do what I'll die doing: ride, hard and fast.

My bike is in sight. I parked it between a couple of dumpsters behind what used to be an upholstery shop, and it stands out like a gleaming black gem, waiting for us. That bike means a hell of a lot more to me than just a hobby. That bike means freedom-- it meant it for me so many years ago, and it'll mean it for this girl, if I have anything to do about it.

"Hey," I murmur as I get to the bike and slowly set her down on the seat. "How we doing? Are you with me yet?"

As I pull the blanket down from her face, I see her mouth moving faintly, but she's still dead weight. I frown. I kept the blanket over her so that anyone glancing my way might not guess immediately that I'm carrying an unconscious woman off, because that's a bad look if I ever saw one. But we're going to have to get on the road if we have any chance of getting out unnoticed.

"Fan out, they're not far!" I hear from down the road in a hoarse shout.

Too late.

"Fuck- hey," I hiss, gently trying to shake the girl awake enough to ride with me. "Listen, if you can hear me, we've got to go, *now*. I'm gonna put you on my bike, and you're going to have to help me help you, can you do that?"

"Mmruh?" she replies, and as I pat her on the arm to try to snap her out of her sleep, I feel her start to squirm.

At least I won't be just draping her legs over the seat and hoping for the best, but I need her awake.

BANG.

My heart jumps to my throat when the gunshot goes off, and immediately, I grab the girl and dive to the ground with her. She isn't awake yet, but that jolts her out of her stupor enough to squeak as we go down together. My body breaks the landing, and my first instinct is to crawl out of the way with her and pull my pant leg up to get my own gun out.

I point in toward the sound of the voices, and sure enough, one of the three men down the road who's closed in on us is the same one I stole the keys from earlier. I fire at them just enough to let them know I'm packing and send them running for cover. That's all the time I need to get us to our feet and check the girl for injuries.

Around the same time that I'm looking her body over, I feel the aching burn in my shoulder through the rush of adrenaline surging through my body. I glance down at my shirt and see the bloodstain growing, and I have my answer. I don't have time to see how bad the damage is. It's mild enough that I'm still on my feet, and if I can do that, I can ride.

I get us both on the motorcycle in a hurry and fire up the engine. When I do, our attackers come out of cover to keep us from escaping, but I'm firing in their direction before they even come out. The man I pick-pocketed takes a bullet to the hip, and I watch him hit the ground in pain before I gun the engine and peel out of the alleyway, clutching the girl's arms around my torso as tight as I can.

The wind whips around my face as I barrel out of the alley in the opposite direction, and a truck leans on its horn as I swerve to avoid it when I jet out of the other side. My bike thunders down the street while I hear more bike engines revving behind us, but I'm so focused that bombs could be going off around us and it wouldn't deter me any more.

I hear a bleary murmur and a tired groan as the girl leaning on my back starts to stir, her strawberry blonde hair whipping behind her. For a second, I hold out hope that that's going to be a good thing for us. But then I hear the distress in her soft murmuring, and for her safety, I tighten my grip on her wrists, pinning her to me.

When she comes to, and I feel her look around her surroundings, I'm glad I'm holding her tighter. She screams and tries to pull back and jerk away at the same time...on a moving motorcycle that's picking up speed *fast*. I lean the motorcycle to keep our balance and grit my teeth as I hear a gunshot behind me. With the girl riding on my back, I can't afford to have them on my tail.

"Ohmygod ohmygod ohmygod!" the girl breathes as she tries to jerk away from me. "Stop, let me off! Where am I? Help!"

"Hold on tight," I growl before I turn my bike around at an open stretch of road, and she screams again as we see what's coming after us.

A pack of bikers at least five strong at a glance is roaring our way, and as I veer to the right between a couple of businesses, I hear more bullets rip across the darkening skies. It's twilight, and the faces are harder to make out--that's good for me, but it won't stop a gunshot.

"Help!" she tries to shout at them, her voice still slurring and clouded by brain fog. But I squeeze her hands and glance over her shoulder enough for my glare to reach her, and it seems to stun her to silence.

"*Those* are the bastards who had you!" I bark. "I'm getting you out of here, so listen--I need you to hold onto my waist tight, and do not let go for anything. *Anything.* Do you hear me? I need you to say *Yes*, can you do that for me?"

My voice is authoritative and clear, giving her a strong, simple instruction to follow. I'd used that voice with civilians plenty of times before before my discharge. If you start barking out orders with force, people usually pay attention--especially if they're already drugged up and fighting that off.

"I-I..." she stammers, confused but no longer trying to jump out of a moving vehicle.

The sound of the other engines gets closer behind us, and two gunshots ring out that ricochet off concrete walls, and I feel her hug me tight, pressing her face to my shoulder. That's as close to a *Yes* as I'm going to get, so it'll have to do.

With one hand now free, I pull around a corner and swing around the building, hugging the side so that I can stay out of sight while I take my gun out. Moments later, the rival bikers fly past the intersection, and I fire two quick shots at their tires. They're moving fast, so I'm surprised when even one of the bullets hits someones leg, and they lay down the bike in the road while the rest of the pack swerves to avoid him.

As they topple, I'm barreling off down the road again.

We need to get out of town, and fast. I know of an old gas station that isn't far from here past the other side of town--I passed it on the way in. But I can't have these fuckers on my tail while I head there. Just then, I hear the sounds of police sirens not far from where I left the pack, and I smile.

"HELP!" the girl shouts when she hears them too, and my heart jumps again as I put my gun away and grab her wrists again.

This time, she jerks and struggles more, and my bike wobbles under the shifting weight. "You're going to kill us both if you keep doing that," I snap. "We've almost lost them, hang on!"

Her heart is pounding so hard as I rocket out of the town that I worry she's going to pass out again, and I can tell how terrified she is. She has every right to be, I suppose, but we don't have time to stop and talk things out yet. I don't know how long I've got until the other bikers are able to shake the cops, or even whether the cops are on *their* side. Diesel has deep pockets, after all.

I ride up to the gas station, whose gas price sign has long since decayed and been broken into tattered pieces by the wind. Weeds grow through cracks in the concrete, and the sides of the walls would be covered in graffiti if there were more than maybe a couple of teenagers in this tiny town.

The girl quiets down as we approach, surprisingly so. I don't question it. I pull the bike around the back and find that the rusty back doors are closed and locked, and the place looks like it hasn't been occupied by squatters.

"This'll do for now," I say, still holding her wrists as I cut the engine next to the doors and climb off and help the girl do the same.

Her body starts shaking immediately once we've stopped, and her face looks ghostly pale. She looks up at me in utter terror, and I know how this must look. I'm a man with at least a head in height over her, and she just woke up to a nightmare guided by yours truly. But I need her to bear with me a little longer.

With no time to chat, I open the bike's storage and pull out the tire iron I keep on hand and carry it over to the nearest window that looks climbable, with the girl in tow. I hold her back before smashing the window in, making her jump and yelp, but I ignore it and move forward to shine my phone light inside. I glance down at the girl to make sure she's wearing shoes, then nod to the window. She looks horrified, but we don't have a choice.

A moment later, I'm helping her up into the building, and I hear her land safely on the other side. I join her seconds later, landing with a heavy thump in front of her. I see the whites of her wide eyes staring up at me in fear as I walk past her to get the back doors unlocked. As soon as they creak open, I wheel my bike into the back room and shut the door, where I can finally breathe.

"There," I say, breathing a sigh of relief. "We'll be safer here for now than we will anywhere else in t-"

I turn around to look into the front of the store...where I see that not only has the front door been unlocked in the ten seconds it took me to get my bike in, but the doped-up girl I just saved is high-tailing it out toward the road at full sprint, screaming for help as loud as she can.

"Fuck!" I snap, and I give chase.

I'm a tall guy who spends a lot of time on his body, and most people don't believe me when they hear I'm fast. Most people haven't been taught how to *really* make their bodies hustle, but I've had to put my body through hell before, and I know how to move. I'm also a somewhat intimidating sight to see approaching at full tilt, because as soon as the girl glances over her shoulder to make sure I'm not following her, her face goes sheet white.

She cowers down on reflex and freezes like a deer in the headlights as I close the distance between her and scoop her into my arms, slinging her over my shoulder while she kicks and screams, trying to fight me off.

"Get off me!" she gasps, more afraid than angry as she kicks blindly.

Lucky for us, she's easier to get under control

than an actual deer in actual headlights. I hear bike engines and spot faint headlights coming from the long stretch of road leading out of town, and I hurry back to the building with her. She grabs onto the door to keep from behind taken back in, but I'm not waiting, and she loses her grip with a terrified yelp.

"Please-" she says as I set her down, but instead of replying, I spin her around, pin her back to the front of my body, and clap her mouth shut as I press myself against the wall. I sink to the ground and hold her trembling form to me as I silently put my hand on my gun and listen.

As the engines get closer, the girl against me stays still, but I can't read her mind. She's quicker than she seems, clearly, and apparently knows how to act fast when she needs to, but the simple fact is that she's been through a lot already. Her body is soft and warm against mine, and the faint perfume still clinging to her hair fills my nostrils as I wait. I close my eyes and clench my jaw, controlling my body's desires. They're an annoying distraction I'll have to handle later.

The engines get close enough that if she were to break free again, we'd be spotted. I gaze down at her while she watches the door, eyes wide. Finally, she looks up to me, and she shrinks away when she realizes I've been watching her. There was some debate in those eyes. I can't trust her, not yet.

But the bikes pass, and when the dust has cleared, we're alone.

"I'm going to let you go now," I tell her. "If you run, you lose that privilege. Understood? Nod."

Her eyes are easy to read, and I see a kind of innocence in them that's used to being trusting. She nods softly, and I'm willing to believe her to show her I want to work together. My hands release her both at once, and she stands up, rubbing the dust from her mouth before wobbling.

I stand up and steady her, but she draws back from me immediately.

"We can't do this all night," I say with a frown, but just then, I hear motors on the road again. The bikers must be coming back into town for the night. *Shit!*

The girl seems to have picked up on this too, and she looks to me as if sizing up her odds of making a break for it. Where she's standing, she has a pretty good chance of making it to one of the doors, too. She'd at least get far enough to get their attention.

"Listen," I say slowly. "I don't know who you are, but I'm a friend. I used to be a soldier. I'm here to help you, but you need to believe me when I say those guys out there are *not* your friends."

"The police are," she counters in a thin voice, surprising me with her courage.

"Maybe," I admit. "But I don't know that in this

town. Those bikers are bad news, and they've got connections."

She seems to understand vaguely what that means, but I can tell by the look of her she hasn't grown up around bikers. Her body is soft, and she looks like she's had a rough few days, but she looks like she takes care of herself. She isn't the kind of person used to this life. It fits Diesel's MO to a tee. There's probably nobody in the great state of Wyoming who even knows who she is or that she's missing from...somewhere. But that makes for a panicked person, and that's dangerous.

"We're going to lay low here until those bikers aren't a threat anymore," I explain, taking a few slow steps toward her. "If you want to live, you need to follow my orders exactly. I don't know how you got here, and you've probably been kidnapped, but not by me. I can get you through this, but I need you to believe me first."

With every step I take toward her, her suspicious eyes only look more concerned, and she backs up toward the icee machines that still have some now-brown sludge in the tanks. She swallows as her butt touches the counter and she realizes she's cornered.

When I'm an arm's length away, she blindly reaches behind her and grabs the first thing her fingers wrap around. "Stay back!" she hisses, brandishing a flimsy plastic spoon at me threateningly.

I raise an eyebrow and smile softly, and she

notices her weapon of choice. "Crap," she whispers, tossing the spoon aside.

I'm amused for a moment, but then I see the tears forming in her eyes. This poor woman really does think she's at the end of her rope with me, and she's too shaken to do anything about it. But she needs my help, and I have to build that trust.

I take a step forward, and she puts her hands out to stop me, but I catch them. Holding her firmly yet gently, I look down into her eyes and let her stare back up into mine in awe. I want to let her search me, to know she doesn't have to cower.

After a silent, tense moment, the red washes over her face, and she lets herself slowly rest against my broad, heavy chest. I wrap my arms around her and holder comfortingly, shushing her as I feel the sobs start to wrack her body.

"What's your name?" I ask quietly.

"Justine," she manages to get out.

"I like that name," my dark voice rumbles. "Call me Ironside."

She looks up at me, apparently not comforted in the least by the name I ride by.

"I know it's hard," I say in a husky growl. "But you need to stay by my side right now, because if you go back out those doors again...your life is over."

My blood runs cold. My chest rises and falls rapidly, my heart pounding like it might just pop out from between my ribs and drop to the floor. I can feel every cell in my body shifting into sheer panic, all the pent-up terror and dread I have been fighting back comes pouring back into me. I feel like someone has taken the moon and tipped its crescent peak to let its shivery glow fill me with light from within. It is an electrical feeling, a full-body impulse I feel almost powerless to resist. The world around me filters from bright colors to muted hues, all movement frozen in space like I'm standing in the sketch box of a comic strip. All is still, all is empty. There is nowhere for my eyes to look than at him.

Him.

Even through the shifting and blurring clouds

over my vision, no doubt a side effect of adrenaline and not much else in my body, I can see the man who claims to be my savior. He is every piece and bit the prince I used to daydream about on those long afternoons in the mahogany pews, my mind wandering toward more earthly pleasures as the preacher pontificated about heaven. I used to think I was bound for that heaven, for that particular brand of paradise. The purest kind, reserved for the best-behaved girls, the prettiest ones with the soft tongue and nodding head. The girls who do as they are told without a hint of reluctance, no stirrings of a self-created destiny. I am meant to be among those chosen few, the brightest white and fullest of the flock. There was a time when I thought I was pure enough. I did what my father asked of me and I thought that was proof enough of my piety and my good intentions. Even when I wanted to cry no, turn away, refuse the smile beckoned for from the cruel curling lip of a man passing me by on the side-walk--I knew better than to let myself slip. The mask I wore, clean and blank and empty, has slipped.

I see around it now, just a little bit. In my muddled mind, he is the center-point. He is the focus around which the rest of reality spins. It all hinges on him. It all depends on what he wants to do to me. I have long since abandoned the hope that a man could want nothing from me. They will always demand something. My time, my attention, my purity, my total servitude.

And this man is a god among mortals. He is larger than life. In the blurry, muted world he still burns like a white-hot brand in the middle of the quiet chaos. Those black eyes fixated patiently on me. There is a predatory tilt to the way he stands in front of me, arms outstretched, one of them still holding my arm while the other beckons peace. His palm is turned to face me, which whispers of a truce. Maybe he does not want to kill me just yet. Maybe he is taking his time. Maybe this one likes to toy with his food before he devours it. My thoughts are slurring from one neuron to the next, incomplete beats and pauses, a Morse code binary I can't quite tap out at the moment. Someone must have drugged me.

"I don't feel like myself," I murmur, accidentally out loud. The coarseness of my own voice startles me. "I don't sound like myself either," I add, coughing.

"Someone did a real number on you," he growls.

I try to summon the muscles needed to nod my head. It feels like gravel rolling in between the folds of my brain, so I stop. I just stare at him stupidly, mouth slightly agape. I hope he will understand me. I hope he can see the truth behind my vacant gaze. Every part of me wants to scream, this is not who I am! This is not what I'm like! Help me! But whatever poison is pumping alongside my blood in my veins has rendered me dumb. Still, I can feel my senses starting to trickle back to me through the deep haze. Smell comes first, even before touch. My nostrils burn with the acrid scent of gasoline pooling on pavement. The sickly-sweet syrup of a grape soda staining the floor inside the convenience store. The familiar chalky sensation of breathing in old dust. Who could tell what kinds of tiny parasites and bacteria make their home here, and now I am just breathing them in. My eyes flick over to the white plastic spoon on the sticky linoleum. Embarrassment hits me like a fly swatter to the eye.

Why did I even try to fight him off? Why did I think I even could? The man before me looks like he could be an angel come to lift me to paradise or a devil sent to drag me further into hell. Either way, lift or drag, one thing is for certain: my time on earth as I have known it is over. I do not belong to myself. I do not belong to my father. And I certainly do not belong to the old man who planned to call me his bride, bought and paid for. But I cannot be a free agent. My daddy always taught me to mind my elders, mind my betters, listen to what the man has to say. If I am no longer my father's property, then to whom do I belong?

He regards me with a hint of concern, like he knows I've got the same panicked impulse as a cornered rabbit in a dark forest. It's fight or flight, but I cannot fight this man and he has already proven that I cannot flee from him. What else is there to do, in this situation, but freeze?

"How did I end up here?"

The words come choking, rasping from my dry throat before I can think better of it. The man's eyes soften, just ever so slightly, and only for a moment. But I see it. I understand it. Something wild inside of me lets itself be tamed. Only for a moment. But long enough. He isn't going to hurt me. Not now, at least. It's less of a conscious assessment, more like a long-dormant instinct lifting its head to tell me this man is my only chance of safety. He is the life raft tossed to me through the storm. I would be a fool not to grab hold of him and hang on for dear life. Finally, I am grateful for his fingers wrapped around my upper arm.

I drag in a slow, deep breath. I close my eyes and listen to my own heartbeat, isolating the thudding sound in the midst of the blaring silence. The scattered pieces of my mind start to come together, mending seams and breathing back to life. I am so deeply confused about how I got to this point, to this abandoned gas station with this dark-eyed stranger with the shiny machine and the roaring engine. But I'm drifting back to earth again. It's starting to become clearer, more real. But with reality comes pain, and I feel a painful lurch in my gut. Hunger, twisted up with thirst and adrenaline. It's awful, but at least it reminds me that I am alive. Maybe that's too low of a standard for what I need to scrape by, but all we can be are the sums of our experiences, and lately my experience of life has been pretty darn traumatic.

The man makes a move to reach for the napkins and I freeze up, tensing my body for... what? For pain? He clocks the split-second look of terror on my face and he adjusts his body language to better suit me. He straightens up his posture and relaxes his shoulders, letting his arm drop to his side. His black eyes watch me closely, almost like he's studying me, measuring my response. I swallow down the lump in my throat and give him a subtle nod. A flex of my slim bicep to give him a go-ahead.

Slowly, he reaches for the napkins again. This time, he grabs a handful of them and turns to offer them to me, arm outstretched. With only a moment's hesitation, I extend my own trembling hand to accept them. I dab at my face awkwardly, my movements stiff and jerky. My whole body is so exhausted and overdrawn. My reflexes feel like they've rusted over. The man watches me swipe at my face half-effectively with the napkin, but to his credit, he doesn't look at me with pity. It's only understanding. He sees me, but he does not look down on me from above. He's trying to do this the right way, it occurs to me. I ought to at least try and meet him halfway.

"I'm... I'm sorry," I mumble, scraping the napkin

at the thin skin under my eyes. Tears well up instantly and spill over. I'm surprised. I wonder how long they've been lingering there, just on the edge. It is a strange sensation, coming back to your body after leaving it.

"Sorry for what?" the man asks, stepping past me with his hand still on my arm.

I turn slowly after to face him. I watch him dodge the sticky bluish-green stain on the floor from where some likely-radioactive slushie syrup spilled.

I clear my throat and say, "I'm trying to get it together. Really, I am."

"Oh, I believe you," he rasps softly. "I only know half of your story, and it's the half that started when you woke up. I have some ideas about what the first half was like, but I don't know for sure. All I'm certain about is that somebody messed you up, and we'd better do whatever we have to do to keep that somebody from getting you back."

"What about you?" I breathe. I blink rapidly, trying to make the world focus again.

He's staring at me. He's wary.

"What about me?" he repeats gruffly.

"Will you let go of me?" I ask, flat-out.

I notice him clenching his jaw. He wants to say no. His instincts say no.

But he tilts his head slightly and murmurs, "Yes. But only if you make me a promise."

Hardly daring to breathe, I ask, "What is it? What do you want?"

"Swear to me that you won't go running out there again," he says. "Because if you do, it could cost us both our lives."

"And you're willing to ask for my word?" I muse aloud, surprised.

"That's what I'm doing," he sighs.

"And my word-- you trust it?" I push him.

He glares at me, those dark eyes penetrating deep into my soul. He shakes his head.

"Frankly, no. Not at all. But I'm going to let go anyway, because I need to grab you one of those sealed bottles of water from the broken cooler over there. Don't make me regret that decision," he hisses.

He lets go of my arm and I almost stumble back a few steps. I didn't realize that I was leaning on him the whole time. His gaze is locked on me.

"Believe it or not, I don't want to drag you around," he says. "Unless you want me to."

It takes a moment for the suggestive nature of his words to sink in, and then I feel a faint blush creep across my cheeks. My heart thuds painfully in my chest. But I manage to croak out another reassurance.

"I swear it. I won't run this time," I promise him.

He pushes back from me, letting both arms drop. I feel like a shackle has been shrugged away from my shoulders, my body feeling ten pounds lighter.

Almost too light. I realize how very flimsy I feel, like I'm a paper doll swaying in the breeze. My savior was holding me down. He was my anchor. Now I am unmoored. But all I can do is stand here and numbly watch as he steps past me and over to the upturned cooler full of bottled waters. I find myself totally fascinated by the ripple of muscles moving fluidly under his clothes. His long, easy stride. His swaggering gait. How his shoulders are so broad, his back so powerful. His hands reach down into the cooler to extract a couple bottles, and I realize with a flicker of something much more than simple interest that he has very large hands. They are calloused and rough-looking, like they have been suited for a life of toil. I wonder what kinds of dirty work those hands have molded to? What lives and bodies and places have those hands touched? Who felt those hands before me? I can only silently wonder.

My heart skips a beat when I realize that his body is facing away from me right now, just for a few moments. He isn't looking at me. His body language does not include me. It strikes like a clanging bell through my mind that if I am looking for an opportunity to bolt, this is the only one in sight. The muscles in my calves twitch, as though begging me to run. The impulse flares up and burns inside of me white-hot for a second or two before dissipating. My feet are fully rooted to the spot. I can no sooner run away from my savior than fight him. I am here now with him for as long as he will keep me. Of course. It's the only thing that makes sense. I can feel myself memorizing him bit by bit, shaping him into some worshipable deity in my mind. I am a girl, and Daddy taught me well to find a man and make him my god, and I will always be protected from the devil's intentions. So I fold to him. I turn myself to face him like a flower tilting back to gaze full-resplendent in the sun.

He twists the cap off a bottle of water and hands it to me. I take it greedily and tilt it back, gulping down impatient mouthfuls of the life-giving drink. It's not until now that I realize just how parched my throat has been all day. I can feel my body cooling off and loosening up, being replenished by the water. It feels like heaven in my throat. I notice that the man is staring at me again, thinking me over.

He asks, "So, what do you remember? Tell me whatever you've got."

I bite my lip and try to open up my wincing mind. I need to remember. It hurts. The memory is painful. But I need to drag it into the light. It starts to come back to me in little vibrant pieces, none of them at all comforting.

"The first thing I remember is stumbling down the highway," I begin slowly. "I was… I was crying. I remember my eyes burned. It was hard to see straight. And I was so scared and tired, like my legs might give out. Then there was a car horn. Somebody honking at me. It rattled me half to death, but then the trucker pulled over on the shoulder of the road. He said he could drive me out of Utah. That's where I wanted to go. So, I climbed up inside the cabin with him."

"Wait, wait. Go back," he says, stopping me. "Why were you trying to get out of Utah?"

"I was running away from my family and my… my obligations," I answer. "I was supposed to be married, you know? Daddy-- my father set it up."

"Like an arranged marriage?" he questions.

I nod. "Yeah. Just like an arranged marriage. To my father's friend. He's fifty years old. My dad set the date for my nineteenth birthday," I rattle off. I sound unemotional as the words come out of my mouth. But it's not me. It's something inside me.

"What kind of monster would set up his own daughter with an old man?" he spits.

I shrug, biting the inside of my cheek to push back tears.

"I don't know! My father is that kind of monster, apparently!" I blurt out.

And as the words fall out of my mouth the emotions start to creep back in, slowly seizing my body bit by bit until I'm crumpling over and nearly falling to the floor. I lean back against the sticky counter by the slushie machine. My chin quivers, my skin prickles up with goosebumps. I was never prepared for this. Any of this. I have lived my life as a caged bird. I am not ready for the world and its worries. I have been kept so quiet and so lonely I never dared to dream beyond the view from my bedroom window.

"I'm a fool. I ran away because I thought there was nothing worse than marrying an old man I don't love," I confess bitterly. "Can you believe it? I thought that was the worst the world has to offer, but I was so wrong. There's much worse. I have no one to trust. He wants to catch me and drag me back, but now I'm here with you and… and you just don't seem like the kind of man my father would have sent after me."

Again, that ugly blare of panic throttled me and I began to hyperventilate. Immediately, the man rushed to my side and took me by the shoulders, peering intently into my face.

"Shh, shh. Calm down," he whispers. "Your father didn't send me. I don't even know who you are. But you have to stay quiet, okay? At least until those fuckers have given up."

I try to nod in agreement, but my eyes lock onto something else that frightens me: blood. Running down his arm. Dripping onto the linoleum square between us. Again, my heart quickens and I start to breathe erratically, fear taking over. It's a bullet wound. He's been shot.

"Shh. Quiet. I'm fine. You have to be quiet," he

urges me. "I've got you. I'm fine. You're fine. We just have to lie low until they move on."

Slowly, my panic ebbs away to a dull throb and I allow myself to fall silent, clutched in his protective arms. I feel almost safe for a moment or two, and it's intoxicating. Not to mention arousing. My body warms and trembles against his and my muddled mind gets confused trying to work out the difference between panic and desire. The wires are all crossed, I'm sure. But what will happen from here I do not know.

It's no longer up to me, though.

It's up to him.

She isn't running. That's a step in the right direction.

"Thank you," I tell her slowly, reassuringly. "How are you feeling now? How clear is your head?"

"Uh..." she hesitates, looking uncertain and failing to come up with a response.

"That's fine," I tell her, nodding and pointing to the counter. "There's counter you can sit on if you want to take a minute while you drink that water-- but do drink that," I add firmly.

She nods, but I don't stop staring meaningfully at her. She blushes and quickly takes another long drink, and I nod.

"You've been drugged for god-knows-how-long," I say. "If you don't drink up now, you're going to feel like shit in a few hours. Believe me, I've seen it plenty of times before."

"How long do you think this is going to last?" she asks softly as she rubs between her eyes on her way to the counter.

"There's a chair back there too, but I wouldn't trust it," I say as she leans against the counter and holds herself. "Don't know, but you're walking and talking right now, so it's just a matter of getting you to sober up. That's the bright side."

"I'm guessing the downside is whoever's coming after us, right?" she asks, eyes flitting to the dark windows.

"Yeah," I admit, nodding. "You look young, but you're no kid, and I'm not going to hide anything from you. Those bikers are persistent, and they're not going to just let us go because we got away. There's going to be people looking for you all over the state, so we need to figure out what the next step needs to be. And that starts with you," I add. "So besides your dad, where's home for you? Who's 'your crowd' and how can I get you to them?"

She clutches her water with both hands and stares at the ground for a long time. Just when I'm about to walk over and make sure she hasn't spaced out again, she sniffs and closes her eyes softly. A tear rolls down her nose and drips to the floor, and I get the message.

There might not be anyone else in the world this girl has besides her relatives, and that sanctuary just turned into...something else.

I can still only barely wrap my mind around what Justine told me about her father. It isn't unheard of, unfortunately. Sure, it isn't the kind of arranged marriage that most people think of, like some old fashioned debutante being married off for land. But out here in the rural midwest, especially further back in the hills where it sounds like Justine must have been coming from...things can get strange.

Those small towns are ruled by patriarchs in tight-knit communities, and some of them have pretty rigid values. And there aren't a lot of ways to protect people who need it in those kinds of living situations.

"Hey, it's okay," I say, nodding my head to show I understand why she's crying and stepping forward. "I hear you. I saw some of that in parts of Colorado. That's where I'm from. You ever been?"

It's a silly question, but I want to pull her mind out of the hole it's digging itself. She nods her head softly and looks up at me.

"We drove through, once," her weak voice says. "It was pretty."

And there's that hollow voice again. I've seen it before. She might or might not be dissociating, just zoning out and going into autopilot while her instincts take care of her in the meantime. It's a defense mechanism. When reality is too hard to face, you just clam up and go inside. I'd seen that look on men's faces enough times before now.

I nod my head when I see she isn't going to say more. Before I can speak again, I catch her glance up at me with a hint of desperation in her eyes. Reluctantly, I open my arms and wrap her in them, holding her to me while she melts against my form and closes her eyes, trying to fight back tears.

She needs someone right now. Bad. And all she's got is me.

There's something else she isn't telling me. I have a nose for that. I don't know what it is, but this girl has some trauma in her past. Even if her choice to turn into a runaway was impulsive, people with good home lives don't do crazy things like that at the drop of a hat. She's been hurt somehow.

I don't mind. I've been burned too.

"You don't have to say anything," I tell her. "I know how it is."

"Do you?" she asks.

"Enough that I'm not going to let you out of my sight until I know you're safe," I promise her, looking her in the eyes sternly. "Understand?"

She nods and swallows.

Originally, the closest thing to a plan I had in my head was to get the girl somewhere safe with her family or friends, then round up the club and burn that fucking club to the ground. And I still have half a mind to do just that, but not until I take care of this girl who has *way* more baggage than I ever bargained for tonight.

None of this is her fault. She doesn't deserve to suffer from the fallout. I just hope having to babysit a runaway isn't going to get us both killed.

While she rests her head against my shoulder and starts to let her weariness get to her again, I take out my phone and write up a quick text to Breaker--our prez. He needs to know I won't be back until late, and that we've got a situation on our hands.

Break bad news early and often. That's one lesson I didn't learn in basic.

I don't think the prez will object to me taking this detour. I'll fill him in on the dirty details when I show up with a girl on the back of my bike, but for now, I tell him that I've got someone who might have valuable information on Diesel and his new club.

That's true enough, too.

I hear her stomach growl loudly right after I send the text, and I smile down at her now-open eyes, which she lowers with embarrassment.

"Tell you what," I say, "there's a diner open all night a few miles down the road. I've stopped there once or twice before. They make a mean patty melt. You like those?"

She looks at me as if that's a tempting offer.

"Alright," I say with a grin. "Let me grab another water for you for the road, and we'll get on our way. Some food will help clear your head, too. Don't know how long it's been since you ate last."

I wheel my bike out of the back, and Justine follows me cautiously, eyes widening at the sight of the bike. She's seen it before, of course, but she hasn't gotten a good long look at it yet. She seems impressed with the sleek, barebones beauty of her, but I'm not the kind of guy who wants to wave his bike around like his dick. I just appreciate a fine machine.

"How did you get me on this earlier?" she murmurs.

"Not easily," I grunt. "I was worried you were gonna blow away in the wind if you didn't jump off like you were trying to."

She blushes.

"Sorry," she says sheepishly.

"Don't sweat it," I say with a gruff smile, glancing down at the hole in my shoulder. "We did what we needed to. Now come on. I've already talked more tonight than I usually do all week."

She hesitates and has a couple of false starts trying to swing her leg over the seat, and I offer her my hand to help support her as she climbs on behind me. She settles in and slides her hands around my stomach, and now that we don't have the pressure of gunmen chasing us, I feel my heart start beating faster at its warmth.

Shit, I was worried about that.

I turn the engine on, and she squeezes me at the sudden vibration under her. It's one thing to hear a motorcycle starting up--another entirely to be on it and feel that beast come to life. I check her hands, then take off down the road.

It isn't long before she rests her head against my back, both to shield herself from the wind and because she's exhausted. There isn't much to look at in this part of the state on either side of the road, so I can only imagine she has to fight to stay awake.

As for me, I'll be surprised if I get a wink of sleep tonight.

Justine. The name keeps ringing in my head, like a part of a song stuck in my mind, but it only makes me more curious about her. She's been through more over the past however-many days than some people do in their whole lives. And aside from that, something about her almost seems to glow. It's like I snatched an innocent little songbird out of a den of wolves.

I can't let myself think about her the way my instincts want. I've never let anyone know that I have a type, but she's it. I barely even know her, but parts of her story hit close enough to home that I don't think we're as much strangers as we think.

But she needs my help, not my loving. And that's what I'm going to give her.

We pull into a roadside restaurant off the interstate and bring the bike to a stop in the cracked parking lot. It's late, but not the time of night that drunks are stumbling in. The crowd looks mostly like truckers and a handful of other workers stopping in for a bite. I help Justine off the bike, then open the back and slide my kutte off.

"What are you doing?" she asks sleepily as she rubs her eyes and watches me take out some gauze.

"First aid," I grunt, casually wrapping the bandages around the wound in my shoulder to get some pressure on it. "It's not bleeding bad, but this'll do until we can get somewhere safe for the night."

"Do you need a hospital?" she asks, eyes widening at the blood under my kutte.

"I've handled worse," I say dismissively. "Besides," I add, looking her up and down. "Don't know how much of outlaw life you've grown up around, but hospitals aren't an option right now. We're on the move."

I decide not to remind her that it's because I put a bullet of my own in at least two men back there.

And they give the two of us a look as we step in.

I furrow my brow, wondering what they're looking at, until I notice Justine. She's on her feet and awake, but nearly falling asleep on the ride and the drug still working through her body makes her look dead on her feet, and both of our clothes are roughed up.

There's also a small patch of a dark stain under my kutte that could barely be made out in the green of my shirt, but nobody needs to know that's from a bullet hole. But we look rough as hell, and the diners don't seem any less uneasy when I nod to them and lead Justine to an empty table.

She sits across from me, and I'm reminded again that she must be ten years younger than me. I'm in my early thirties, fit, and rough around the edges. She looks twenty and like she's been drugged and tossed in a basement.

Heartbreaker kutte or no, this doesn't look great. I'll have to bank on the diners having seen stranger shit in the past.

"Can I get you two some waters to start off?" a waitress asks as she bustles up to our table, trying to look less concerned about the situation than she was.

"That'd be great," I say. "And a coffee for me. Justine?" I ask her, wanting to let the waitress know the girl and I are on a first name basis.

Anything that makes me look like less of a kidnapper will do.

"Just water," she says with a weak smile before looking to me. "Do you mind if I get cleaned up in the bathroom? I...won't be picky," she says in reference to the menus in front of us. "But I'm hungry."

"Sure thing," I say with a gruff smile, and I watch her get up and smile to the waitress before making her way to the bathrooms.

When I look back to the waitress, I see that all mirth has left her face completely. She's staring down at me with brazen suspicion, and sigh as I roll my shoulders back.

"Couple of patty melts," I grunt. "And two eggs. And bacon. Side of hash browns."

The waitress wordlessly jots the order down and heads off to the kitchen, leaving me to crack my neck and glance back at the bathroom impatiently. As soon as she gets back, I'm planning to have the loudest, most conspicuous conversation as I can get away with about how not suspicious the two of us are. Maybe I can even get Justine to laugh, that would do the trick.

What doesn't scream *funny guy* about the name Ironside?

But when enough time passes that our food arrives with no sign of Justine, I start to worry. I wish I had a burner phone on me I could have handed her, but I just have to wait this one out. I don't want to make them even more suspicious of us than they already are. Justine is in bad shape though, and letting her out of my sight already hasn't gone well.

"'Scuse me, ma'am," I say in my most professional soldierly voice, making her stop and look to me before leaving the table. "This all looks great, but I'm worried about my friend back there."

"Sometimes women take a little time, hun," she says curtly, obviously thinking that the girl wants some time away from me.

"She's not well," I say more seriously. "I mean, you saw her when we came in, didn't you? She's feeling faint, I just want to make sure she's okay."

The waitress looks reluctant, but finally, she nods and leads me to the back of the restaurant and raps on the door.

There's no answer.

The waitress knocks a few more times and calls the girl's name, and when she gets no answer, she curses under her breath and takes out her keys.

"There's no window in there," she murmurs as she turns the lock and pushes the door open, and I step past her to get inside.

Justine is sprawled on the floor, out cold.

JUSTINE

*E*verything is chaos. The world around me is a swirling black abyss, and I cannot for the life of me figure out if it's night or day. A grim voice in the back of my mind informs me that it doesn't matter. Either way, it's the same for me. I am in the dark place, and here the rules by which normal people live their lives are bent and twisted. Nothing makes any sense here. Nothing is logical. I can't tell which way is up and which way is down. It's like my thoughts are a tiny metal ball in a pinball machine, and every few minutes, the board gets all shaken up. My train of thought moves slowly, sluggishly. Molasses through bog water. I want to move, to regain the power in my limbs to control my own fate again, but it feels impossible. Every part of me is so heavy, so weighed down with languid exhaustion. I wonder what they have been doing to me. I wonder how they have managed to scrape out my soul and separate it from my body. Because that is how it feels. Like I'm being torn in a thousand different directions and I can't find due north. My internal compass is spinning like mad. Where am I?

And in the context of this whirling darkness, who am I?

Because the version of myself I used to know is gone. I am being erased, my personality deadened with drugs and torture. How can I remember the bright things when the dark is so full, so penetrating? I keep trying to get my eyes to focus, my consciousness to come back to life. But whatever they did to me... it was potent. I don't understand how I got to this point. All I know is that it only gets worse from here. They're hurting me. Or maybe it just hurts all over because my heart is broken. Because the one thing I know for sure is that I was betrayed. I have been perverted and subverted by the very man who was supposed to protect me above all else.

My father. He is the devil who brought me to this particular ring of hell. He is the liar and the pretender who lulled me into a false sense of security and then used my acquiescence to his advantage. I have to hand it to him-- his plans fell into place so perfectly. I realize now, even through the thick fog surrounding my brain, that he has been preparing me for this my whole life. He is the one who made me soft and pliable. He is the one who taught me to say yes, to do exactly as I am told even when I don't want to. He led me down what I thought was the golden, shining path to eternal purity and safety. If I just preserve myself, if I keep myself whole, then I will dance forever in the gardens of heaven on earth. What a pack of lies. Here in the darkness, the lies burn brighter than anything else. They're a neon flashing sign, reminding me of just how easily swayed I have been. But then again, I was made this way. They want me this way. It only makes their job easier. I don't know exactly what they have planned for me, but I know it's not the pure, sunny world they promised me.

The snakes have led me into Eden, but the gardens are turning brown and dying with every moment I spend here. How could I have been so foolish? So trusting? I should have known better than to ever trust a man, not even my own father. But the scripture… it told me to listen and obey. Women are meant to be seen and not heard. Little girls can aspire to nothing greater than the eventual service to a man. I was promised milk and honey if only I did as I was told. But whatever they gave me does not taste so sweet. There's a persistent bitterness lingering on my tongue. I wonder if that's the drug they gave me. Or maybe this is just what betrayal tastes like: charcoal and sawdust in my mouth. I can feel a cold, hard floor under my limbs.

My bones ache down to the marrow. I feel violated and intruded from all angles, like no part of my body or soul has been left innocent. They have taken everything away from me: my life, my hopes, my dreams. My assumption that I would continue along the same safe-- if a little dull-- trajectory I was set upon like a wind-up doll from the start of my childhood. I did everything I was supposed to do. I have been the good girl they told me to be. The scripture shaped me like rivers smoothing a stone, and I have allowed it because I thought it was my ticket to paradise. Nothing hurts so badly as the realization that I was wrong all along.

There is another flavor in my mouth joining the palate of bitterness and regret: a mineral-y, metallic taste I slowly register as being the distinct taste of blood. A flicker of fear passes over me, and with it comes a wave of powerful nausea that threatens to bowl me right over with its intensity. I wonder whose blood it is I am tasting. Reason dictates that it is probably my own, and while that is horrifying enough, it terrifies me even more to think it might belong to someone else. And that is possible. Improbable, maybe, but still possible. Especially because I know for a fact I am not completely alone in here. There is someone else suffering here with me in the darkness. I can hear a soft whimper, a sound similar to the whine of a dog who has been struck by a vehicle. My muddled mind hands me a memory, one so frayed and stained with the passage of time that it's more of an impression than a full recollection. The neighbors had a dog. A little mutt with wiry hair and a crooked tongue. A name surfaces in my thoughts: Rory. Rory the dog. I remember her whine as she lay broken in the road.

I want to say her name. Rory. But it's not a dog crying in the room with me. It is a human woman, and she is in pain. I can feel it, the heat and the agony twisting around her. I try to reach out through the void and close the space between us. My eyes can see her, but only barely. She is a folded-over slump in the shadows of the corner. I wonder what they have done to her. I strain my eyes in the dark place and just barely make out the pale glow of her limbs. She's bunched up like a broken accordion, and she is crying. Tears slick the floor under her filthy cheek. I am horrified by what I can see, but even worse is the knowledge that I might as well be looking into a mirror. She is me. I am her. We are together one and the same under the thumbs of these men who seek to hurt us and take out our souls. Where are we? It's a hell on earth, but it still has to have an address, right? But my brain is too confused and panicked to come up with coordinates. I'm somewhere on earth and I am suffering, but no god reaches to lift me out of torture.

I blink desperately in the low light, trying to let my vision adjust. I make a concerted effort to drag myself across the room. I need to get closer to the other woman. I want to touch her with my soft hands, reassure her until the whimpers soften and go away. The need to give her comfort in this lowest hour is so powerful in me that I manage to scoot a few feet, even though it's like the connection between my soul and my body has been snipped. It takes all of my power just to move an inch. I get the bizarre sensation that I am not really here. That this is an ugly dream, hideous in its accurate portrayal of real life. Why can't I dream of something good? Someplace better? Why must I return here, to this room, of all places? I never wanted to be here in the first place. I have escaped it once, but now I know that this hellish prison exists not only somewhere in the world, but inside of me. The parasite is in me even now, devouring me from the inside out as I struggle to remember and forget at the same time.

"Help me," whispers the other woman. Her voice is weak. Fading.

I want to help her, but I can hardly move. I am so far away from my body. I can feel the life seeping out of my companion's body. She is drifting away, her soul getting so small and so swamped with pain that it can no longer power her body. She is dying right in front of me, and there's not a damn thing I can do to stop it. Tears prickle up and burn in my eyes. I am totally helpless. I am totally afraid. Because I remember something else now, something that frightens me down to my core.

A warning. A threat.

If I do not obey what these men ask of me, I will meet the same dark fate as the other woman fading into death across the filthy floor from me. It is a punishment for daring to deny what the captors ask us to do. She has been silenced for breaking a rule. For fighting back. These men don't want difficult captives. They want easy, soft girls who bend like branches. They will fracture us again and again in pursuit of their own pleasure and their ugly profit.

It is all starting to come together in one narrative. Daddy wanted me pure, not so that I can reach for heaven with my gloved hands, but so that I am an unmarred product on the shelf. He wants a doll without blemishes, a smooth canvas upon which to paint the filthiest colors. Brick red like rust and blood. Pale white like color draining from a fearful face. All my years of protecting myself and guarding what I was taught to believe is my most precious gift-- all a waste of time and hope. The high road ends here, in the darkest ditch. I'm angry with myself for even believing him in the first place. I let him brainwash me. I let him own me. And for what? Only to end up in the ownership of someone else?

Another alarm bell rings in the back of my mind and I realize there is a sound piercing through the dark. It's a voice, an ugly one that makes me flinch. I don't understand what the man is telling me, only that his tone is hateful. Poisonous. My skin crawls to hear the timbre of his voice, imperative and boastful. He knows I am completely helpless. He knows he is in full control over me. I hate it. I want to fight back, but I know there's no point. They have invaded not just my mind but my body, too. They injected me with something that makes my skin burn. Some kind of evil pumping through my veins and rendering me limp and lifeless as a doll.

It isn't until I can feel the wind whipping through my hair, cold and playful, that I start to wake up from the drug-induced fog. A weight lifts off of my shoulders as it dawns on me that I'm no longer in that wretched little cell. I can smell fresh air now. I hear the nocturnal insects singing and screeching in the night. There's something hot and vibrating between my thighs. An engine rumbling like the grumbles of a giant. My body is pressed up against someone else's, making me feel safe and protected. The warmth of that feeling is formidable, a worthy opponent to the fear that captivated me before. I smell something other than the night air. Something more man-made. The spicy scent of cologne burning my nostrils and enticing my body. It makes me feel all warm and tingly inside. My mouth salivates at that smell. It's like black pepper and musk, autumn leaves and cinnamon. It reminds me of crackling fires. Warm places. Silk soft under my bare skin as the sunlight streams in to gently rouse me. A veritable bouquet of old feelings resurfaces in my mind. There is so much to consider, so much to sort through. The scent takes me on a journey and whisks me away from the grim scene I found myself inside.

But those memories are not current. They are old. Irrelevant, right? Whatever is happening to me right now is something totally different. It just gets so hard to sort it out. All the events are jumbled up on top of each other like a ten-car pile-up. What happens when and whose grasp is around me? The delicious scent starts to fade away, being slowly replaced by something much less pleasant. I wrinkle my nose and pull away from the scent of chemicals and filth. What is it? Where am I? I have to get out of here. I have to escape. I can't be here anymore. It makes me sick to my stomach. It's like disinfectant mixed with pungent orange peel and clove, a powerful symphony that still is not quite enough to cover up the stench. People have come here and relieved themselves for years. This place holds onto the bad things. I can feel it.

And then I feel something else entirely: hands. Large, calloused hands with broad palms and deft fingers landing on my body. They are the anchors that tether me to consciousness. I drift back and back and back until I'm closer to my body than I have been all this time. Hands, stroking my face and smoothing down my sides. Firm and waking. My eyes flutter open and I realize with a jolt that everything I have been seeing has been in my own mind. A fluorescent light flickers urgently overhead, and as my vision swims back into focus, there is something looming over me. A human head, a handsome face, framed utterly by the golden-white light like a halo round the precious head of an angel. A guardian angel, by the feel of it. He is here to rescue me, but from what? And how?

Either way, I can't help but lean into him. I manage to wake up enough to slither my arms around his thick, muscular body. I hold onto him tightly, curling in his embrace. His hands push the hair back from my face, stroking my cheek gently. The softness of his touch nearly moves me to tears. It's a welcome departure from the manhandling I have endured in recent days. He doesn't want to break me. He is holding me together in one piece. I have the worry that if he lets go, I will splinter into pieces and never come back together again. So I cling to him desperately. I won't let go. I can't. He bends down to whisper something soft and ticklish against the shell of my ear and his warm breath gives me shivers.

"Are you okay?" he asks gently.

I shake my head, tears trickling down my cheeks. "I'm so scared," I choke out.

"Come on," he urges me. "Let's stand you up and

get you back to the table, okay? You have to eat something or you're just going to keep collapsing on me."

"I'm not hungry," I whimper as he lifts me up.

I brace myself against him as we get right-side up, and I realize we are in a public bathroom-- and a fairly gross one at that. I shudder to think that I have been lying down on that filthy tile floor. But my savior slowly leads me out of the bathroom, back to our table. There are plates of food there, but I'm too foggy to even recognize what it is. The waitress comes flouncing over in her apron, a ballpoint pen tucked behind her frosty curls. She has a look of concern on her face as she approaches.

"Sweetheart, you doin' alright?" she asks me in a low voice.

"She'll be fine. It's just been a long day. She needs to eat," I hear my savior tell her.

"She looks messed up," the waitress says. "You sure she's okay?"

"Yes. We just need some time. And privacy," the man says emphatically.

The waitress seems unconvinced, but eventually she walks away.

"I'm serious. You need to eat something. Can you do that for me?" he asks me softly.

"I...I can try," I murmur, reaching for the utensil.

Fork or spoon, I can't tell. But my captor grabs it for me and starts trying to feed me bites of food. It's something savory. A little salty and soft. Potatoes, I think, with other vegetables mixed in. I can hardly open my mouth to accept the food. Suddenly, there is a hand holding mine under the table. Warmth spreads through my whole body when I realize it's his hand. And he's looking at me with such intensity. He's clenching his jaw. His body is tense.

He's listening for something. Waiting. He turns to me with a piercing gaze.

"Can you trust me?" he whispers.

I want to say no. After all I've been through, it's the answer that makes sense. But somehow, for some reason, I murmur, "Yes." I do trust him. For better or for worse. Something deep inside of me tells me I should.

"Okay. We need to leave now," he instructs, his voice barely audible.

He slides out of the booth and takes my hand, pulling me up to my feet. I'm a little wobbly, and the room spins as he leads me out of the restaurant, a gigantic dollar bill left on the table. We stumble across the parking lot to the motorcycle. We climb on, his arms holding me up. But before we can even start moving, there's the sharp wail of police sirens. Cop cars come whirring into the parking lot, and the waitress is pointing at us accusingly.

The motorcycle roars to life and the chase begins.

"Step off the vehicle, put your hands in the air!" one of the officers barks as I feel Justine's grip around my waist tighten.

I can almost feel her heart pounding against my back through my bloodied kutte. Her fingers clutch my shirt. The panting, terrified breathing from over my shoulder is almost a comforting sound compared to the boots of officers approaching us.

"What do we do?" she whispers. "God, I'm so sorry!"

"Wasn't you," I say under my breath. "I don't think these are the good guys."

Keeping cops on the take might as well be on the first page of the playbook for outlaw motorcycles. Whether for better or for worse, the serious biker gangs keep their law enforcement officers close by, and they keep an ear out for anything suspicious.

We have cops of our own back in our town. When the mayor or some other fuckhead land developer threatens the honest townspeople, we pull the strings we have to in order to keep them safe. If the cops won't do that on their own, we'll do the same, because Heartbreakers don't wait for someone else to do the right thing.

I never do. That was what drew me to them, and that's probably going to be what puts me in the grave in this kutte some day.

Today isn't that day. I'm not about to go down by one of Diesel's bought cops for Justine to get thrown right back where she was. And I know these small town types--the wrong man will do anything for a paycheck.

The officers are out of their vehicles, slowly walking toward us with their hands on their guns. Justine watches them with a white face before looking to me.

"Don't put your hands up," I say to her quietly.

"*Get off the bike and put your hands in the air, now!*" the same officer shouts again, getting ready to take that gun out of its holster. "Step away from the woman!"

"He's with me!" she shouts, but I nudge her with my elbow.

"Don't give them anything," I warned her. "Even if you don't think it's incriminating."

"Then what's your plan?" she hisses.

"Hold on tight," I say.

"What?" she breathes, just as the cops get about five paces from their cruisers.

I gun the engine.

The sound of my motorcycle roaring to life and peeling out of the parking lot gets peppered with the shouts of the officers as hell breaks out. Virtually all the diners have their faces pressed against the window to watch me screech away from the cars and into the road, where I hang a sharp right just as I hear gunshots pop off behind me.

"Fuck!" I cursed as I heard the sounds of squad cars roaring out of the parking lot after us.

Cool, dry night air whips over my face as I charge into the near pitch blackness of the long road at night. Clouds are giving us good coverage overhead, which is as much a help as it is a problem.

As soon as I'm out of the town, I cut my lights, putting us in true darkness and prompting Justine to squeeze me again while the sirens wail behind us.

"What are you doing?!" she asks.

"Keeping us under cover of dark," I shout back over the wind, barely audible at speeds well over a hundred. "If they can't see us, they can't find us."

She doesn't seem all that comforted by this, and to be fair, neither am I--animals run out onto the roads all the time, and I'm liable to run into something or hit a pothole and end this chase real goddamn fast. But it's a choice of either running that risk or definitely ending up dead.

I can see it all too clearly: the police gun me down as a fugitive, Justine disappears, and the news might run an article about some outlaw kidnapper tied to the Heartbreakers died in a kidnapping attempt.

Getting caught isn't an option tonight.

We're locked into a chase with the police, and I'm now a wanted man in what I'm quickly realizing is Diesel's territory, whether or not we realize just how it's moved and expanded. I knew that stealing this girl right from under Diesel's nose would be like taking a baseball bat to a hornet's nest, but I didn't think I'd rouse the cavalry.

Lucky for me, Wyoming is all straight roads, and a bike outruns a squad car any day of the week. But it's not that easy. If it were, adrenaline wouldn't be coursing through my veins and letting me think and act as fast as it takes to escape the police.

"Are we outrunning them?" she blurts, looking at the shrinking red and blue lights behind us growing farther away every minute.

"Yeah," I bark. "My bike *goes*. But in an hour or less, they'll have a blockade up ahead of us if we can't figure something out. We need a place to hide out."

"We picked a great place for that," she shouts with a hint of sarcasm as we blaze past endless plains of barren wasteland on either side, only dotted by a few hills here and there.

She has a point, of course. Just because there weren't any lights ahead didn't mean it would be like that for long, and we'd have to figure out what little hiding territory there is and work with it.

But in the meantime, while we race forward and scan the landscape around us every time a break in the clouds gives us a little moonlight, the adrenaline has a chance to stagnate, and the reality of tonight starts to set in.

I just stole the most beautiful woman I've ever met from our biggest rival himself, and now, I've got half the county police after me. Pretty little girls like Justine don't go missing without causing a stir in the news. Then again, Diesel might want to keep her identity quiet if he can.

It's too early to know just what the consequences will be for what I've done, but I don't regret a thing.

There was a time in my career when I couldn't save someone, even when I did everything right. Some stories from my younger years I plan to take to my grave. I'm not letting myself go back to that place again. Justine isn't going to slip out of my fingers. I'm going to take care of her even if I have to drive her halfway across the damn continent and beyond.

I'll keep riding until I see a light at the end of the tunnel. Nobody deserves what she's been through. It doesn't take anyone special to recognize that, just a decent human fucking being.

"Do you see that?" she calls into my ear, pointing far ahead of us.

It's a light at the end of the darkness alright, but I grit my teeth.

Fuck. I know what that formation of headlights means.

"Those are bikers," I shout. "Diesel's men, most likely, none of my club is riding out here right now."

"What?!" she croaks. "Are the police still behind us?"

"Do you want to stop and find out?" I shout back, grinning.

"No!" she says, not in the mood for jokes.

"Too bad," I call, "because that's exactly what we're going to have to do."

I point ahead to a large hill coming up on our left that has just enough of a slope on the other side to give us some cover from the road. There is a little brush dotting the hill that makes me hold out hope we'll have somewhere to post up and wait.

When we're finally close enough to the hill, I quiet the engine and guide it to the side of the road slowly.

"Why are we stopping here?" she asks as soon as it's quiet enough that she doesn't have to shout. "I can still see the biker headlights ahead of us!"

"And we should start to hear the cop sirens

before much longer too," I say, nodding as I help her off the bike and start wheeling it off the highway. "We're between a rock and a hard place, and there aren't many options to hide. So we have to use this to our advantage."

"I thought you said the bikers and cops were working together?" she says as she trots after me, and I start to hear the white noise of nighttime in the wilderness all around us.

"They might well be," I growl. "But it's dark, and none of them are going to recognize each other like this. If we're lucky, they're going to see bikers, and they're going to lock onto them. The only thing we have to worry about is whether or not they're going to collide on top of us or not."

She nods her head silently and plods along beside me. I glance over at her periodically, and I can tell that she's at least alert, but it's almost like she's in shock. Her movements are stiff, she keeps staring off into the distance, and she doesn't look like she's totally awake on the inside. The poor thing needs a proper place to rest.

All I can offer right now is the next best thing until we get back to the clubhouse.

"Here," I say as we wheel around to the other side of the hill, which has a much steeper slope, to my relief. "This should keep us out of sight."

"How do you know they won't look for us?" she asks, holding herself tight.

"I don't," I admit. "But this hill doesn't look different from the dozens just like it we passed on the way up here, so unless those pigs want to stop and root around every half mile they pass, we just need to hope they haven't had eyes on us somehow."

I bring the bike to a stop by a patch of brush, and after beating around it to check for snakes, I take out a thick military-issue blanket from the back of my bike and nod to a relatively even patch of dirt near the bike. I spread it out for her while she watches, holding herself. She shivers a bit, and I know the chill of the open air at night must not be something she's used to like I am.

"Here, take a seat," I offer, patting the blanket for her.

"Are we just going to...wait?" she asks, anxious.

"Yeah," I say bluntly. "And this seat is just going to stay cold if you don't take a break. We've been riding hard, and you're not used to that."

"Should we keep our voices down?" she asks, stepping forward cautiously and slowly lowering herself to a seat on it.

I pick up the back edges to fold and drape over Justine's shoulders, wrapping her up in a bundle. She draws it close around herself on instinct, which surprises me. The blanket looks a lot like the type I found her in, so I was worried at the last second that she'd be uncomfortable, but she seems to need the warmth.

She seems to alone on her own, though, and the way she stares ahead of her doesn't help. The girl has been through a lot, and building trust has already been a...rocky process, at best.

Considering we've only known each other a few hours, I'd say we're doing alright.

"Hey," I say in a low, husky voice as I crouch down beside her. "Keep that blanket tight around you. You're going to need all the warmth you can get. You're not dressed for riding.

I sit down beside her, and I'm surprised when she leans into me automatically, as if she didn't even have to think about it. There's a moment of hesitation before I feel her soft body truly relax into mine when she feels how warm I am.

Without a word, I wrap an arm around her and give her a gentle squeeze.

"You're doing great," I tell her softly.

"I got the police called on you," she says, clenching her eyes shut.

"Don't give yourself too much credit there," I say, mostly for her benefit. "That waitress could have called the cops on anyone who looks like me with a girl, not just because you were there. Not that she wasn't justified, I suppose," I add with a sigh, wondering whether Diesel had really gotten his claws into this county yet and how deep his pockets ran.

She doesn't look like she totally believes me, and

she shivers again as we start to hear the sounds of bike engines getting closer. She looks up to me, and my heart melts. I want to give her space, but she seems like that might not be what she needs right now.

"Come here," I offer, spreading my legs and nodding for her to scoot into me.

She gives me a bewildered look, but I open my arms. "Keep low against me while we wait them out. It'll keep you warm, and we won't risk sticking our heads out at the wrong time."

Despite her reluctance, she doesn't need much convincing. She scoots between my legs and slowly rests her back against mine while I lean us back and press us to the hill at the angle of the steep slope. It feels like hiding out in a war-zone, and it makes me all the more protective of the girl in my arms.

"How's that?" I ask softly.

"Good," she murmurs, a single syllable that warms up my heart better than a bowl of chicken soup.

I feel a smile tug at my lips, but the bikes are getting closer.

"Stay down," I order her gently. "Do you have a happy place?"

"Huh?" she asks.

"Somewhere you can go in your head," I say. "Somewhere safe. Now would be a good time to find it."

She bites her lip, then nods and closes her eyes, taking a deep breath and letting it out slowly.

The bikes get closer, and I swear I can feel the rumble of them in the earth under me. I move my hand while I listen. I try to make it feel to Justine like I'm just reaching to scratch, but I'm keeping a hand on my gun, ready to draw it and do what I have to do if the bikers find us.

"I'm going to take you somewhere safe after this," I tell her, squeezing her gently. "You're not going down tonight, little one, and neither am I."

She squeezes my shirt softly before I hear the bikes roar past us at last.

They fly by as the sirens get closer, and I watch them rocket past us right into the line of cops heading our way. They probably think they'll just be passing the cops like any other group of harmless riders.

But when the bikes are long past, I watch their headlights fly into the red and blue flashing sirens of the police, chaos seems to break out, and I watch the lights start to chase each other back toward the town.

And all I can think about is whether or not they'll turn around...and how good Justine feels pressed against me.

The night air is cool and refreshing as it billows softly across my face. The night birds twitter and hoot. The insects sing their scratchy hymns in the underbrush. The moonlight is thin and pale, casting the earth in a pale, sickly glow. But I have my own compass, my own focal point to keep me grounded to this planet even in the face of such horror and confusion as has settled down around me in recent hours. The man who has come to rescue me from an uncertain fate still holds me steady as we crouch in the brush. Every faint movement of his body makes the leather jacket he wears give off a buttery scratchy sound. It's oddly comforting, like the sound of fresh linens folding and crinkling under one's cheek. I have my arms wrapped around my hero's powerful, muscular body, and underneath the flat palm of my hand is his heartbeat. I feel it thumping, slow and rhythmic, strong and steady. The sensation is calming, as my own pulse slows to meet him halfway. My fear slacks and falls back.

He makes me feel safe, like nothing bad can really happen to me as long as I am by his side. In his embrace, no harm can come to me. He will fight off the demons. He will protect me. At least for now-- at least against these particular enemies. I am safe here as long as he is with me. I still don't understand why he is protecting me. I mean nothing to him. I mean nothing but dollar signs to anyone, even my own father. My self-worth has never been so low, but my savior's attention makes me feel a faint flicker of my old confidence. I have never been boastful or prideful-- my upbringing never allowed for anything like that. I'm just a girl, after all. The best I can hope for is to make a pretty bride one day and gladly give myself over, mind, body, and soul, to a man.

But he doesn't seem to want anything from me. Nothing I would not gladly offer, anyway. At this point, he can take his pick of whatever I have to give. He has rescued my body from a dark end, and I will owe him my everything for that. Even if we don't survive this bloody night, I soothe myself with the prospect of dying in his strong arms. If I can no longer dream of a beautiful life, then at the very least let me have a beautiful death.

Then again, the cops are looking for me.

Growing up, I was always taught that the police were a force for good, that they would protect the innocent like me. But what if I am not so innocent anymore? Will they still fight for me or have they all turned against me?

I am so confused. My thoughts are moving slowly, and everything that happens is too fast, too hard for me to comprehend. My body is tired. I fantasize about falling into a pile of soft sheets and pillows. I crave oblivion. I want to sink into the darkness and let my limbs lose their strength until the soft night folds in around me like the arms of a princely lover.

Maybe, though, I should stop hoping for a prince. Maybe it's a knight I need instead. Someone with a bright and shiny sword rather than an ill-gotten crown. I need to be somebody's queen, not their princess. I need to be strong for myself, but he makes me weak. I cling to him tightly, afraid that if I let go for even a second, he will disintegrate and leave me all alone in the cruel world. I can see the cops roving around, their flashlights beaming the grass and pavement as they search for me. A little instinct inside me beckons for me to run to them. To confess my sins the way I have been taught to do. I have never been good at hiding the truth. In my upbringing, a lie was as unforgivable as a murder. A falsehood as ugly as a bloody knife. I know that it's my training to bend to authority, to submit to a uniform.

But there's something about the cops that gives me pause. I swear they seem all too familiar, like I recognize them from somewhere. And it is not a positive memory-- that much I know at least for certain. I can't remember from where I've seen them. Or maybe I just don't want to remember. Either way, I stay put. I simply watch the lights dance across the road and the field where we crouch hidden. The sirens wail and scream, making my heart race faster. My savior holds onto me, his body curving around my much smaller frame. He is protecting me, shielding me from the police. My reflexes are so muddled. Everything in me wants to run to the cops and throw myself prostrate before them, beg for forgiveness, plead to be taken home where I belong. But I have to remind myself again and again that I don't belong anywhere anymore. Daddy hurt me. My home is no home now. Just an empty shell echoing with false memories.

The sirens are starting to fade, the flashlight beams clicking off. The darkness is nearly uninterrupted now, and I feel my savior's body start to relax ever so slightly. He is pleased. This is what he hoped would happen. It worked; we stayed still and silent and the cops are moving on, returning to their vehicles to continue the chase in the wrong direction. As soon as I think it's safe to speak, I gather the courage to whisper to my captor-cum-savior.

"Please. I just want to go somewhere safe," I murmur, my voice barely louder than a sigh. "Will you take me away? Just to… to a motel or something. Anything. I need it."

"Safe is a relative term, little one," he says grimly. "You're naive if you think you'd be safe at a motel."

Tears spring to my eyes. I know he isn't trying to be unkind. He just does not want to lie to me. I can appreciate that on some level, vaguely. At least he is telling me the truth. After a lifetime of eating up lies, I should be grateful. And I am. But I'm also terrified, and desperate for some kind of reassurance.

"You can protect me," I mumble. "I'll go wherever you take me. Just… take me away from here. Please. I need to rest."

"Be patient," he whispers, stroking my hair.

I fall silent and lean into him, listening intently. The cops have moved away now and so have the other motorcycle riders. The road is free and empty, the air quiet except for the distant echo of rumbling engines. We wait for a while in the cold darkness, even longer than I expect. The sounds are gone for quite some time when we finally stand up to walk the bike back to the road. I lean on my savior's strong, muscular arm as we make our way through the tall grass, the wheels trundling through the mud.

"Coast is clear," he says. "Come on."

He lifts me effortlessly and puts me on the motorcycle, then climbs on in front of me. By sheer instinct, my arms fall down around him. I lock my fingers together interlaced around his barrel chest. I can feel his taut, defined abdominal muscles, his bulging pectorals and biceps. He is a wall of pure strength and raw endurance, and I find myself clinging to him like the last life raft in a storm. He settled into the motorbike seat and put his hands on the handlebar, gleaming in the moonlight. I saw his knuckles going white as he revved the engine to life and we began to putter down the highway. I am completely exhausted, every muscle in my body aching and strained. But I cling to him for dear life, as though his strength is enough to support us both. I hope that's true. I certainly don't have enough of my own strength left intact to rely on. Every now and again, Ironside touches my hands, tracing his fingers over my locked hands, my aching wrists. Every touch feels like the hand of god on my body, and I find myself starting to calm down despite myself. What kind of magic does this man possess?

Whatever is the source of his power, it is the very thing I have been searching for all this time. I have been floating around this world in a daze, never fully connecting with anything. I suppose that isn't entirely my fault. My father has done a very thorough job of keeping me locked away in my ivory tower, kept innocent and naive so that I am soft and easy for the world to fold over. He made me this way. He made me weak. I'm sensitive. Every cruel touch is like fire on my flesh, burning me up into ash. But this man in front of me, revving the motorcycle down the lonely, fearful highway, is different. He is exactly what I have been hoping to find, or rather, what I hoped would find me. When I ran away from home, I dreamed of running into a guy like this. Maybe he's not fully the old-timey prince I imagined. He's rougher around the edges, frayed and stained with time and blood. He can take care of me, though, and his gritty experiences only make him a more formidable protector.

He is just what I wanted, if I am to look past my modesty and admit to myself what I really need, what I really desire. I long for someone to protect and take care of me. I sure don't know how to look after myself. My father made sure of that. He wants me frail and lost, unable to stick up for myself. He wants me utterly vulnerable. But Ironside is my armor. He treats me the way I want, not the way that horrible old man treated me. The man who was meant to be my husband. The thought alone makes me want to vomit. He is too old. Too cruel.

But Ironside is perfect-- older and wiser than me but still close to my age. His body is broad and menacing. He's a powerful force to be reckoned with, but he has still shown me so much tenderness. So much softness. He guards me like a sword but he touches me like silk. I have never experienced anything quite like it, and I doubt I ever will again. He's something special, and for the night at least, he is mine. And I am his.

We ride along the highway for some time, and my mind is too clouded with fog to know how long it has been, but after a while we slow down. The engine dulls down from a roar to a pleasant purr and we gently roll down a slope into a darkened parking lot behind what looks like a shutdown bar. But I can hear faint noises coming from within which inform me that it is not actually closed down-- it just looks that way from the outside.

"Where are we?" I ask softly as we roll to a stop and he cuts the engine.

"Somewhere safe. Just for a moment," he replies. "But you are going to stay here and wait for me, okay?"

I hold on even tighter, fear flaring up inside me. "I don't want to be alone. Please take me with you," I plead.

"I won't be long," Ironside assures me.

He detaches from my desperate grip and slides off the motorcycle seat. I watch him walk away, stalking toward the back door of the building while I tremble and quake alone in the dark. But I can't stand it. I hate being out here alone. I feel so vulnerable. So I do something I have been taught absolutely never to do: I disobey a direct command from a man.

I slip off the motorcycle and start creeping my way across the parking lot, careful to keep my steps so soft they make almost no sound at all. Once I reach the door, I slowly push it open bit by bit, seeing the wash of light from within. I slither inside, sighing with the onslaught of warmth that rolls over my body. There is a positive, wholesome feel to this place. It is filled with love and light and hope, and I am immediately hit with the desire to lie down and rest. But not yet. I am on a mission. I have to find Ironside so I won't be alone anymore. I never want to be alone anymore, not after what I've gone through.

I creep along a hallway, keeping close to the walls. I follow the sound of uplifting voices, people just casually chatting and cracking jokes as though everything was okay. It's an enticing noise that draws me out deeper into the building. I know it's a risk, but I just want to be safe. I want to be where the bright voices shine. I want to be around smiling people again. I peer around a corner and see a broad room with yellowish lighting-- a bar. There's a long, glossy mahogany counter where several bar stools are aligned, occupied by smiling faces and hands gripping cold beers. My mouth waters at the smell of booze in the air. I don't drink-- it's against the rules. But I'm so thirsty and desperate that it actually smells good to me. At the bar, I am distracted by four people in particular: two women and two men. Ironside walks up to them and the breath catches in my throat.

One of the men is speaking in a conspiratorial tone, trying to convince the others of something, though I don't know what at first. I strain my ears to listen.

"Okay, now, don't get me wrong: I'm a man of my word. But I'm just saying, maybe this time you could cut me some slack," the man says, grinning from ear to ear as he talks to Ironside.

"You do this every time, you know," quips another of the men.

"No, I don't!" the first guy says, clearly offended. "It's just that--"

"You suck at pool but you never turn down a game," interjects one of the women.

"Or a bet," adds the other woman.

"Sounds like you brought this upon yourself, eh?" the second man says.

"Will you all just let me speak?" the exasperated guy says.

"Go on, then. What's your logic for not paying out this time?" Ironside asks gruffly.

"I'm just saying, I am singlehandedly responsible for that last shipment of bourbon," the guy retorts, holding up one finger for emphasis. "And since Ironside goes through that shit like it's water, I think it just about evens out, you know?"

The others seem very much not convinced. I stick to the shadows as I watch them talk and debate among themselves. The ground floor of this place appears to be a regular biker bar, though I get the sense that there's something much more involved going on here. I watch as Ironside pulls the second guy aside to chat with him more privately. He lowers his voice and looks very serious. I strain to hear what he says, but I only catch bits and pieces here and there.

"Found the girl."

"What's the situation?"

"Not good."

"They follow you?"

"Tried to."

The man turns and looks at one of the pretty women at the bar for a long, heavy moment. Then he looks back at Ironside with an expression of resolve. "Well, you know the drill. Whatever it is you need, you got it in spades, my friend," the guy tells him.

Ironside claps the guy on the back and turns back to walk out of the bar. My heart starts to pound as I realize he's coming to collect me-- but he doesn't seem to expect to find me outside. In fact, his black eyes are locked on me. I realize with a jolt of fear that he's known all along where I've been, just hiding in the shadows. How stupid could I have been to assume he wouldn't notice me? He still has the generosity to pretend to be surprised as he saunters over to me. Even so, I can't help but flinch in expectation of pain or punishment as he approaches.

But to my even deeper surprise, he doesn't punish me. He doesn't raise his hand against me. In fact, he gives me a soft smile and says, "I have a place for you to stay. And clean clothes."

I see both of the women from the bar get up and walk past us to head out. They each offer me a cautious smile as they pass. The other two men stay at the bar, whispering in low voices to one another, looking serious. Meanwhile, Ironside takes me by the hand and leads me upstairs to a small private room. By this point I am so exhausted the rest of the events happen in a blur. I sit down dazed on the edge of a bed. Ironside walks around, setting things up for me. One of the women comes upstairs to offer me some clothes that clearly belong to her. I think she says her name is Kate. Then, the other woman, who calls herself Lauren, brings me some food. I'm too tired to even fully register what it is, other than edible. I pick at it halfheartedly.

"Okay," Ironside says, jolting me and getting my attention as he stands in the doorway. "You're all set up here for the night. I'll be just down the hall."

I look at him with wide, pleading eyes.

"Please. Don't leave," I beg him. "Stay with me."

I'm hesitant, but damned if that offer isn't tempting.

She's looking up at me with those doe eyes I spent all damn day keeping safe, and now she won't leave my side. I can't deny that she's been through more than enough to warrant a pair of eyes watching her for the night, and I trust myself to do that better than anyone else. But still, she's as vulnerable as she is fragile right now--at least, she seems to be.

I can't pretend I know this girl, but she needs a friendly hand tonight.

"Come on," I finally say after some thought. "I'll show you downstairs."

Her tired face grows into a smile, and I hear her footsteps behind me as I turn and head to the stairs. We have rooms down there where some of the officers stay--mostly the core bunch of us who've been with the club so long we were here when Breaker first bought out this basement and Kate started sprucing it up.

Now, it's a nice little speakeasy tucked away under a biker bar. It's perfect for us.

Justine seems to appreciate it on the way down, too. At least, she looks happier with it than the last bar where she was being kept, so it's an improvement.

"Do you own this place?" she asks.

"Down here? No," I say. "I rent a place in town, but there's a room for me here when I need it."

That was kind of an exaggeration. I'm here about half the time, truth be told, and the room I'm leading her toward is mine, plain and simple. Anyone in the MC would say so. I don't want her to think I'm posting her up in my own place so I can keep her under lock and key. Sure, that's part of why I'm putting her there for the night, but all I want is to keep her safe.

...even if the thought of her in my bed makes something stir deep inside me.

I can't let my mind wander down that road, but she makes it hard not to. I can't deny that I'm attracted to her. It would be impossible not to be. Despite her smaller frame and her youth, she has held up through more than a lot of men I know can't. And there's something about her stride that keeps drawing my eyes, and I can't put my finger on it.

You don't make it as far as she has without a little fire in you, and she has that in spades. The copper undertone of her hair is proof of that, I think with an amused smile.

I open the door and show her what looks like a humble, very clean room with a simple but spacious bed and a wardrobe. There's also a footlocker containing some of my old military things, but I keep that locked and out of the way. "It's not exactly a five-star hotel," I say, "but it's comfortable. And it's safe," I add, nodding down to her. "That much I can promise you."

To my surprise, she has a smile on her face when she steps in. She surveys the room, and I suddenly become much more conscious of my living space. Her eyes seem to linger on the faint imprint of my head on the pillow, the tattered old book on my nightstand, and the folded and organized clothes on top of the wardrobe waiting to be put away.

She's taking in the room and learning things about me in ways I'd never have thought of. She has sharp eyes. Whatever her impression of everything is, she seems more at ease in here than anywhere we've been to so far, and that brings a smile to my face.

"Think it'll do?" I ask.

"Thank you, so much," she says with a tired smile.

"Is...there a bathroom down here where I could get cleaned up?"

"Yeah, of course," I say, nodding and jabbing a thumb out the door. "Use the private bathroom just two doors down on the left. Oh, and here," I say, walking to the drawer to take out the most comfortable shirt I own, shaking it out and holding it up for her. "I don't exactly have pajamas here, but if you want something to sleep in besides what you've got..."

I trailed off as her eyes widened--the thing looked absolutely massive in comparison to her. When her lips smiled and a pink blush came over her cheeks before she laughed, my heart melted. Still, she took it from my hands and clutched it.

"Thank you--again," she says.

I give her a silent nod as she hurries down the hall, and I run a hand through my hair.

"Shit," I murmur under my breath. I don't know where that little lady has been, but she's had it rough.

While she washes up, I run to another bathroom to do the same for the grime on my face and hands. She isn't back when I return, so I take the time to change into a clean set of clothes. I kick off my boots and change pants and socks, but when I pull my shirt off, I'm reminded of my injury with a painful twinge. It's been aching all night, but I'm used to pushing pain to the back of my mind.

With Justine around, that's even less of a problem than usual.

I sit down on the bed with my first aid kit (an essential, for any MC clubhouse) and remove my shirt to start removing my bandages and cleaning the wound properly. My face is stony at the sight of the hole in my bare shoulder, and I start to take out a little bottle of alcohol when I hear a gasp at the door.

Justine is standing there wearing my comically oversized t-shirt...and not much else, by the looks of it. After a quick rinse, what was already a stunning face looks fresh and even warmer than before. I'm struck to silence at the sight of her. Her curvy body looks delicious in my shirt, where those hips will be rolling around in my own bed before long.

Damn, that's too far. I can't think like that about her.

The surprise on her delicate features turns to worry a second later, and she glances out the door before coming in and shutting the door. "Oh my gosh, I forgot about that! Are- are you okay?!"

I chuckle and glance down at the hole. "This? I've slept off worse."

She doesn't look convinced, so I beckon her forward with a hand. Her cheeks turn a faint pink for some reason, but she obeys and pads over to my side.

"I hate to ask," I say, "but I need to know if you see one or two bullet holes on me."

I expect her to be a little squeamish, but she reaches down to take the bottle of alcohol from me and does the same with the cotton pad on my knee before checking over the wound with concern. "Two," she says as she brings the wipe to my skin and starts to clean it.

"I only got shot once," I say, nodding. "Bullet comes in, bullet goes out. I'd know by now if the damage was serious. I got lucky."

"Lucky," she says with a faint laugh. "Understatement of the year."

"Luck's just about the only thing that really delivers, I've learned," I say.

"I'm starting to understand why," she says as her hand brushes around my wounds.

Once I'm cleaned, she dresses the wound with gauze, and I can tell she's worked with it before.

"Ranch family?" I ask.

"No," she says, "but my hometown is a long way from the hospital. It's hard not to learn a little first aid growing up."

"Bullet wounds?" I say, raising an eyebrow.

"Nothing that exciting," she admits.

"Exciting, huh?" I say, and I glance back at her when I feel her not move for a few seconds.

Her eyes seem to be drifting along the length of my back, but they snap to mine when she notices me, and she sits down on the bed, blushing and turning her head as she scoots to the center.

"Sorry, I'm just zoning out a little," she says with a weak smile as she pulls the covers back and crawls in.

"Don't sweat it," I say with a warmer smile, looking at my bandage. "Feels great. Thanks, you didn't have to do that. I'll get you some water for the night," I say, standing up and taking my shirt from the end of the bed.

I hear her murmur something like a sleepy thank-you from behind, and I grin as I pull my shirt on. By the time I sneak back into the room with a full glass of water, she seems to be fast asleep, her head nodding off to the side.

I decide to keep watch over her tonight. I've got a comfortable chair in the room, and I've stayed up overnight more times than I can count. The military changes the way you treat sleep--I'll get it when I need it, and until then, I'll make do.

She turns over in her sleep as I get settled, and my eyes watch the outline in her body as my cock starts to stir. I wipe my hands over my face and grab my book from the nightstand to let my mind wander in more chaste directions through the night.

But within minutes, I'm just staring at the pages and thinking over the night.

The Heartbreakers can't keep up like this. We're keeping up with Diesel, but only barely. I could have gotten ambushed in that town if I'd been less careful, and we should have known about his operation there before it even got off the ground. It makes me feel sloppy. I don't like that.

Breaker knows what he's up to, but Diesel himself has gone dark. We don't know if he's planning something big or running scared. The man's like a cockroach, he keeps turning up in the worst places and just won't die.

While that's stewing in my head, I notice a twitching from the Justine-shaped lump on the bed. I can see her face now, and her brows keep furrowing as she shifts uncomfortably. I hear a whimper from her, and I realize she must be having a nightmare. I step over to her and gently reach out to put a hand on her shoulder and shake her awake. She seizes up with a sharp gasp and clutches my arm in terror.

"Wh- huh?" she asks blearily, turning and gawking up at me before slowly releasing my wrist-- which both her hands have to wrap around.

"Bad dreams?" I ask, holding her water toward her.

A hand slithers out of the sheets to take it, and her hazy eyes look up at me gratefully before she drinks, but she doesn't look that comforted. When she sets the glass down, she bunches the sheets close to her and lays her head sideways. The next moment, I see the tears welling up in her face, and I bend down just in time for the sobs to start coming.

I hold her tight against me and shush her gently,

stroking her arm as she hugs me and curls into my body. I feel her tears stain my shirt as she trembles, and I give her hand a comforting squeeze.

"What'd you see?" I ask.

"I...I dreamt about a dead girl," she murmurs, eyes clenched.

It takes me a few moments to realize I heard her right.

"A dead girl, Ironside," she repeats in that flat voice, gaze flitting up to me. "Back at the club. I-I could see her eyes. God, they were so empty."

"Did you see yourself?" I ask.

She shakes her head, and my heart sinks into my stomach. I have a feeling this might not have been a dream at all, but I don't want to agitate her any further. That leaves my own anger to boil under the surface, though. Diesel's operation has claimed many lives, and if Justine had stuck around to piss off the wrong customer...I don't want to think about what might have happened to her.

I hold her while she sobs, and all I can do is support her while she lets it out.

"That's not going to be you," I assure her in a low, husky tone.

"Maybe it should have been," she murmurs, making me frown and take her chin to turn her head up to look at me.

"None of that," I chide her gently...yet firmly. "You deserve to live, Justine. Don't tell yourself any different. I've been down that path. You're not going to like what's at the end of it."

She seems to be paying attention, and she looks almost embarrassed, but she nods.

"I'm not blaming you," I say. "You've been through hell. But you'll heal. How long have you been with Diesel?"

"I'm...still not sure," she says. "What's the date?"

"The 4th," I reply.

"Already?" she says, eyes widening. "I left Utah a week ago, so...less than that."

"Good," I say. "I'm glad I caught you early. You don't want to know what could have happened to you otherwise. You don't have to worry about that anymore as long as I can stand," I told her firmly. "If you don't have people, I'll be your people--and I can protect you...if you want it."

I mean every word, too.

She stares up at me with a searching gaze, as if she's trying to figure that out for herself. Her face warms into a smile, and she cuddles closer to me, so I guess she found what she was looking for in my eyes. I'm surprised to feel her thighs brush against mine, and she pushes a foot against my leg as she stretches and snuggles against me.

"I'd like that," she says softly.

She's too naive to go this alone. I could have been a menace just as evil as Diesel, just stringing her along this whole time, and she'd have played right into my hands. I know people can be empathetic, but I can't imagine she can read minds with those deep eyes of hers.

But I'd like to read hers right about now, I think as I feel her hips brush against mine. My cock stirs, and its ache reminds me how long it's been since I've had a warm welcome for it to sink into. By the way Justine's home life sounds, I have to assume she's never been with someone else before. She doesn't know what she's doing.

Or does she? She's sharper than she lets on. I've learned that the hard way.

Her nose is half-pressed into the pillow, a smile on her face as she breathes in and squirms against my side, supposedly still just getting comfortable. It's like she feels comforted by the things that have my scent hanging on them, from my shirt to my sheets. I could give her a lot more than that for comfort. If she wants it, she probably needs it, bad.

No.

I suddenly disentangle myself from her, gently enough not to scare her but firmly enough for her to know I'm serious. I stand up and look down at her like a disapproving father as she gazes up at me, blushing.

"Kate keeps some tea for sleep behind the bar," I say. "I'll make you some. It'll put you out for the night."

The corridor is dark, and I flick the light on to

get out the electric kettle from under the bar and start preparing tea. It takes about a minute for me to get the feeling that I'm being watched.

"You should stay in bed," I say without turning around, watching the water slowly heat up. "Your body needs the rest."

"Do you think I'm pretty?" she asks bluntly, and I turn around to see her staring at me as if the question is quite serious.

I stare her down for a few seconds, then chuckle and slowly approach her, until we're only a few inches apart.

"You are," I say, showing the most restraint I've shown in the past decade. "And you're going to make someone very happy one day, when you're older."

"I'm nineteen!" she says with a defiant edge in her sleepy voice.

I'm starting to see where that rebellious streak I sensed lies.

"Exactly," I say. "You're clever, but I've got about a decade of experience on you, and right now, you need someone who can help you, because those plains aren't going to be kind to you on your own, little girl."

She takes a defiant step forward and glares up at me. "Are you calling me naive?"

"I'm trying to help you?" I say, tilting my head to the side.

"Look, I'm not some...nun from a convent," she

says, showing that boldness again that I can't help but admire, even if it was brash. "I know what was going on back there. I know they were going to force me to have sex with people for money," she says so matter-of-factly that I barely hear the kettle boiling behind us.

After carrying this wilted flower around the plains like I did, I'm stunned to hear her talk like this. I'm not angry about it. If anything, I'm more curious than ever.

"You've got some spirit, considering what you've been through," I say, turning my back on her and stalking toward the kettle to pour the tea and stir it with a spoon.

"Just because my family was...strict..." she says uncomfortably, "doesn't mean I'm stupid." She crosses her arms, and I can almost see her trying to hold back a smirk as she says, "In fact, Daddy sent me to boarding school for a few years when I acted up at home. I'm no stranger to discipline."

I'm puzzled by why she has that look on her face until it occurs to me that she's been brought into the grittiest biker bar she's probably ever seen, and she's trying to entice the one that took a bullet to the shoulder and is still making her tea. Is...she trying to impress me?

"Alright, rebel girl," I tease her as I carry the tea back to the room, and she pads after me. "Drink this and get some rest. You'll have a clear head in the morning, and we can go from there. Don't flex your rebel streak until then," I say, winking at her.

"I'll be good," she mutters, slipping past me and sliding back into bed to start drinking the tea.

But after sipping it, her eyes go back up to me with that mischievous light in them.

"Where are you going to sleep?" she asks, and I narrow my eyes at her.

"Chair," I grunt.

She looks at me with a silent plea in her eyes, drinking from the warm tea that cast a veil of thin, wispy steam over her eyes.

"No," I say preemptively.

"I don't want to sleep alone, Ironside," she whines, clutching the mug. "I...I think I'll sleep better knowing someone's next to me. Seriously. It'll remind me I'm not...back there," she finishes uneasily.

I know it's against my better judgment, but I can't deny those eyes a request like that, deep down. Begrudgingly, I move to the bed, and she delightedly scoots over to make room for me. I have to admit, caving to her and seeing her happy for it makes it all the more tempting.

She finishes her tea, then curls against me once more with a contented murmur. Her warmth presses against me, and the way she's twisting, I can tell what she wants. I wrap my arms around her slowly, and I feel her whole body seem to relax in blissful peace.

Even though I'm fighting every nerve in my body, it's truly warming to know that this girl can feel so safe in my arms. I may not get a wink of sleep tonight with her ass pressed up against my cock--brat--but it's worth it.

It's good to know I can still make someone feel safe.

I feel so warm and cozy and safe for possibly the first time in years. I am curled up under the sheets with my cheek resting on the soft pillow, Ironside's arms draped around me protectively. I can smell his musky scent, masculine and slightly spicy. It's like the world's most divine cologne, and it's all him. I sense every ripple and twinge of his muscles as he dreams, and I can't help but wonder what he's dreaming out. What kind of harrowing adventures does his mind get up to when the lights are out? Does he dream of someone? As far as I know, he could have a wife or a girlfriend some-where waiting for him to come home. I can just picture her-- flowing long hair, wistful eyes, a white dress. Standing on a front porch, watching the street with a powerful sense of longing. If he has a girl, she must be missing him something fierce. I have only just met Ironside and I already feel attached to him. On top of that, the idea of him being with some other girl makes me want to be sick. It isn't even just jealousy-- it's pure dread. In such a short window of time I have somehow managed to get so wrapped up in his charm that I don't want to imagine spending a night without him. This is the first time, but I hope with every shred of soul in me that it isn't the last time. I want him here, always, holding me and keeping me safe.

My eyelids are slowly starting to droop again, feeling heavier than a bag of wet sand. The room is darkened and everything is quiet except for the faint, muffled conversation from the bar area above. Their voices mingle together, making the words unintelligible and the tones unreadable. Every now and then I catch a little flicker of laughter, but beyond that, it is out of my comprehension. A voice in the back of my mind urges me to stay awake, to stay alert. To pay attention to the voices upstairs and watch for any signs of trouble. After all, I'm not out of the woods just yet. In fact, I have no way of knowing whether I am truly on a path to safety and stability or not. My world has been so violently rocked from all angles that it's hard for me to tell what's good and bad. For example: the handsome, powerful man gripping me protectively in his strong arms right now seems to operate on both sides of the moral compass. On the one hand, he rescued me from an undoubtedly evil operation. That would make him good, right? But then, he seems to be on the opposite side of the police, and I grew up being taught that the police are a force for good and safety and logic. Now, I may be sheltered but I'm not a complete fool. I know police are just people, and people can be good or bad. But that doesn't make it much easier to pick out the good from the bad.

My instincts are screaming at me that this is a good place to be. That I have never been safer than I am here in Ironside's arms. It certainly feels warm and inviting. And strangest of all, it feels natural. Like I was meant to end up here. Something about our union seems divinely-ordained. Like fate itself intervened to bring him to me and vice versa. I can see our individual paths when I close my eyes, watching two serpentine trails winding through the wild, dark woods until they meet at a crossroads, from which we left the forest altogether and levitated hand-in-hand up to the stars. The fantasy softens and smoothes out and I feel the exhaustion sinking deliciously into my limbs and dwelling there. My body loosens up as I wriggle back against Ironside's broad, muscular chest. All logic and reason fall away as my smoky, sleepy dream world settles in like a thick fog. I drift off to sleep, secure in the knowledge that I am safe as long as he is holding me.

I dream of a darkened room, the acrid stench of

pain and suffering burns like acid in my nose. I try to draw only shallow breaths, wanting to avoid sucking in all this filthy, tainted air. I can hardly keep my head above water. It's so humid and dank and dark in here I might as well be at the bottom of the ocean. Goosebumps cover my entire body, and I feel utterly exposed, totally vulnerable. I hate this place. I never thought I would see it again, but here I am. I feel so detached from my body, like I'm watching myself from across the room. I'm a curled-up, fragile pile of skin and bones, melting into a puddle of tears. It breaks my heart to see myself this way. But then something changes-- a shaft of blinding white light beaming into the room. Illuminating my body as though with a glow from within. I watch as I lift my head and make eye contact with myself. But there's such a troubling look in my own eyes that I stumble back out of the room, jerking back from the doorway with a frightened instinct. The door slams shut and I whirl around to find myself in a wide open field of tall, swaying grasses. The wind whips and curls around me as I try to find the moon above to light my way, but the sky is flat black and starless. I begin to breathe heavily now, my heart beat picking up as my hands begin to sweat and I feel nausea in the pit of my stomach. I spin around in place, the darkness becoming so thick and impenetrable I can almost grab it with my hands. The night presses in on my throat and I begin to hyperventilate, pulling and tugging myself in different directions in a vain attempt to escape.

And I must be pulling hard, because I suddenly jolt back to consciousness to find that somehow, I have managed to roll out of Ironside's arms. I'm lying a foot away from him in the bed, my legs fitfully twisted up in the slick sheets. I'm sweating all over, my heart still racing like crazy as the remnants of my dream slowly slither away and are forgotten again. I glance over at Ironside and watch him for a moment, following the soothing, steady rhythm of his powerful chest rising and falling. In the low light, I can just barely make out the hard outlines of his muscles, his sharp jawline and rounded cheekbones. His face and body are resplendent to look at, even in the near-darkness. He is one hell of a man. Everything about Ironside is big. Everything is bulged and strained, even now as he rests comfortably in the bed.

Part of me wants to snuggle up closer to him and force myself to drift off into rest again, but there's another part of me, much more persistent, that urges me to get up and go exploring. I do feel a little antsy and restless. I don't know where I am or why or how, but maybe under the cover of night I can do a little reconnaissance and figure it out. At least find some clues about the nature of the people who are taking care of me here.

So, slowly, I begin to inch my way out of bed,

careful not to disturb the flat mattress with my pointy elbows or knees. The last thing I want right now is to wake up my captor-slash-savior. As much as I crave being in his presence and feeling safe as a result, I know I'm wide awake now. I need to get moving. There's an electrical impulse guiding me as I scoot out of bed. My bare feet touch the cool floor and my toes curl instantly, but I gradually adjust to the cold and push myself up into a standing position. I look back at Ironside, worried that the shift of my weight in the bed might wake him. But to my relief, he seems just as deep asleep as he was a moment ago, and I heave a sigh, clutching a hand to my chest. I begin to pad across the wooden floor, creeping along on tiptoe so as not to wake him. I manage to reach the door and take my time turning the doorknob to reduce the squeaky noise it makes. I push the door open just wide enough to slip through but not enough to let a big pillar of light shine in. Once I am safely out in the hallway, I press alongside the wall as I move toward the stairs. I can hear voices up there and I find myself suddenly desperately curious as to what they're discussing. I move under stealth, my footsteps barely more than a soft tap on the floor. As I climb the stairs, I pass what looks like an antique clock hanging on the wall, still in working condition. It informs me of how late it actually is, definitely late enough for the bar upstairs to be closed for the night. And yet, there are still voices there, which tells me this is no regular bar. This is more like a… a home. Or a commune. Maybe a clubhouse of some kind.

I creep up the stairs one at a time, the voices getting louder and less muffled with every step. By the time I reach the top, I can make out two distinct voices. Both male. There's a strange sliding or shuffling sound, too, which I quickly identify as the sound of a deck of cards moving around. They must be playing a game. I slink along the wall and peek around the corner into the bar area. Sure enough, there are two men sitting at a table lit by only a flickering candle, playing cards laid out on the table in front of them as well as fanned out in their hands. They are speaking in low voices, every now and then smirking or chuckling about something. I wonder why they're doing this in the middle of the night, but then it dawns on me that the card game is probably just a means of wasting time while completing the real work of keeping guard. They're on the graveyard shift, playing a game to keep their bodies awake and their minds sharp.

"You going to keep tabs on this one?" asks one of the men in a low growl.

"Come on, man. It's the witchin' hour. No rules," the other jokes.

"I don't care what the clock says, if you lose, you lose," insists the first with a laugh.

I try to sneak a little closer, squinting as I

approach them. I stick to the shadows, of course, not wanting to be spotted for fear that they might be angry to find me here snooping around. But of course, as my luck would have it, I stumble over a loose floorboard and fall against the wall with a thump. My blood runs cold as my whole body freezes up. With eyes wide, I watch the two burly men set down their cards and glance around, wearing grim expressions.

Oh god. I'm in trouble.

But to my surprise, when their eyes finally fall upon me lurking in the shadows, they seem to immediately soften. One of the men, the younger-looking one, even gives me a soft nod and a smile. As though he's silently relieving me of my worry. They don't care that I'm here. I'm no trouble to them at all. In fact, they look kind of amused to see me here. Like they think it's funny that I'm creeping around their clubhouse like a little shadow. Neither of them makes any move to come stop me or tell me off for wandering. It dawns on me with a warm sunniness that I am not being held prisoner here. These are not my guards meant to keep me in-- if anything, they are keeping the cruel world out. I feel oddly comforted, and as I slink back down the stairs to bed there's a faint smile on my face. The first real smile I have felt pull at my lips in quite some time.

I tiptoe back to the door of the room where I left Ironside sleeping, feeling a lot lighter and less frightened than before. But as I walk up to the door, I feel my heart skip a beat to see that the door is wide open, even though I left it shut. My heart beats faster and my palms get sweaty as I slowly, carefully approach the doorway. As I get closer, I can see the light falling across a serious human face, staring at me with anger.

"Oh no," I murmur breathlessly as Ironside reaches for me.

He grabs me by the shoulders and whirls me around, closing the door behind us and flicking on the light. He pins me against the wall, those dark eyes peering intently into mine. I can feel his breath hot on my skin, the heat radiating off of his body. His fingertips dig into my shoulders as he looks into my eyes. He looks both angry and concerned with me.

Even through the fog of anger he's beaming into me, I can't help but feel a little hot and dizzy as he looks at me. His body is so close to mine. I can smell his masculine scent. I can feel the raw power emanating from his stocky frame. He could so easily hurt me. Hell, he could snap me right in half if he so desired. And as I stand here totally at the mercy of his power, I feel a flicker of something filthy, something I have never really given name or breath to, deep inside of me. Arousal. Desire. His manhandling only turns me on in a way I could never explain. I feel guilty and embarrassed and breathless all at the same time as I wait for my punishment.

"Where did you go?" he hisses into my face.

"No-nowhere," I stammer, barely above a whisper. "I woke up and I went upstairs."

"Did anyone see you?" he asks.

I hang my head with guilt. "Yes. Two men. An older one and a young one. They're just playing cards, though. I promise I didn't interrupt their game or anything. I saw them and then I came right back down," I explain hastily.

"Did you say anything to them?" he growls.

I shake my head. "No. No, of course not."

"Did you go outside?" he throws at me.

"No! I promise, I didn't do anything bad," I plead with him.

He looms over me imposingly, those black eyes sizing me up, testing my testimony for lies. After a few tense moments, he seems to relax a little. Without warning, he reaches for me, scooping me up into his arms. I let out a little yelp of surprise as he flicks off the light and effortlessly carries me back to bed. He lays me back down and pulls me tight against his chest. But from the moment my head touches the pillow, the only thing I can think about is how hard and hot his body feels against mine. I can feel every glorious inch of him, and it's irresistible.

I can't help but roll my hips, subtly grooving my

body back against him. I need to be close to him-- as close as two people can be. I don't understand the urge taking over me right now, but I do know I am helpless to fight it. I need him close. I need him touching me. It's like an itch I have never tried to scratch before, a sickness I never allowed myself to cure or even treat. But by now, so much time has passed. So much in my life has changed. All I want now is some kind of release. I need it badly, and even though I don't understand how any of this works, I am desperate for Ironside to touch me the way I long to be touched.

"You're playing with fire here, little girl," he hisses against my ear, sending shivers down my spine. "Don't light the fire if you don't want to get burned."

"What if... what if I want to get burned?" I murmur back, heart pounding.

"You're barely more than a child. You're vulnerable. You're innocent. You don't know what you're angling for," he growls.

It's true. I don't know what I'm asking for, but I know he can give it to me. So I continue angling for it, rutting back into him, teasing him with my round, taut, little ass. Before long, he's groaning and arching around me, sliding down under the sheets. I suck in a deep inhale as I feel his fingers hook under my panties and tug them down my legs. I lift the sheets to look down at him in wonder. He breathes me in deeply, savoring my lustful scent. My heart races like mad and I'm filled with terror, but I can't back out now.

"Do you even understand what you're asking of me?" Ironside purrs as he slides down between my legs. I blink back tears, even as my body warms to him.

"Truthfully, no," I admit breathily. "I don't understand any of this. But I just need something... a little something to help me fall back asleep."

He wrenches my thighs apart and dips down to suck me in, relishing the way I smell, the softness of my pink petals unfolding under his ministrations. He has me right where he wants me, but he's teasing, pushing me close to the edge before he even touches that secret, forbidden place between my lips. I'm already blushing and heart a-fluttering when he smooths his hands up along the silky skin of my inner thighs. His hot breath is so tantalizing, I can hardly wait.

He pauses, though, looking up at me with those dark, mysterious eyes.

He peers up at me with a question reflecting back to me in those dark eyes. I'm holding my breath, not even daring to move for fear that I might shatter the delicious illusion in front of me. His hands are on my thighs, gently squeezing them, digging in his fingertips in a way that I know will leave tiny purple bruises. Instead of scaring me, this knowledge only serves to turn me on even more. I am afraid, but that fear is balanced out by the overwhelming rush of desire flooding through my body. I want him. I want everything he has to offer me, even if I'm not totally sure yet what that is.

"Tell me, Justine. Do you know what you want tonight?" Ironside growls in a low voice.

I can tell it's taking every ounce of his self-control to hold back right now. If it was up to him, he would have devoured me by now until there was nothing left of me but a shivering husk. He licks his lips and my body tingles with need. I can't help imagining what that tongue would feel like against my sensitive little bud of nerves at the top of my flower. I have only occasionally dared to touch myself there in the past, and even then it was only for a moment. I have spent my whole life terrified of what would happen if I ever give in to the urges rollicking through my body. It's like a drug, this adrenaline-soaked fire of lust that burns low in my belly. I look at him and a desire makes itself known. It strikes and flares so that I can't ignore it. I can't put it aside. He's going to touch me... there. And I am going to let him.

Oh god. What would my father say?

But Daddy isn't here right now. In fact, he might be the reason I ended up here in the first place. This is all his fault, but I am going to reap as many rewards out of this as I can, starting with my captor's tongue. I want him to taste my desire, to memorize my special flavor and keep it filed away in his memory forever. I want to make an impression on him, just like he's already left an indelible mark on me.

"I just want... I want you," I murmur, too embarrassed to say what I mean.

Though to be honest, I don't even know what I mean. But he pushes me.

"You have no idea, do you?" he rasps.

I bite my lip. "I'm trying," I admit in a mumble.

"I suppose I'll just have to teach you," Ironside says.

"Yes," I blurt out. "Please."

He parts my thighs and dips down, breathing me in as my body arches and curls to him. His hands gently grope my thighs, moving down closer to my pussy and then moving away again, teasing and tantalizing me until I'm whimpering for more. I watch with wide eyes as he puts a pointer finger in his mouth and pulls it out with a wet pop. Then he lightly runs his fingertip along the center of my soft, fragrant flower, making me shudder with pleasure.

"Oh wow," I gasp.

He chuckles darkly. "I've barely gotten started."

He leans in and spreads me open, flicking his tongue around my clit. Sharp flames of desire and ticklish pleasure shoot up through my body and I tip my hips up to meet him. His mouth opens and he sucks at my clit, sliding the hardened tip of his tongue around my clit and up and down my slick folds. I can feel myself getting wetter and wetter, goosebumps popping up on my skin as the sensation takes me for a ride. I rock back and forth, letting his warm, wet mouth open me up. My body tenses and relaxes in equal measure, all arching to be closer to him, to that velvet tongue licking me up into whipped peaks. I groan and mumble nonsensically, tears of pleasure burning in my eyes. My hands reach out on either side of me to grab fistfuls of the sheets, holding on for dear life while Ironside begins to move faster and harder, aggressively devouring my sweet cunny. He sucks me up like I'm the antidote to some deathly poison, like I'm the most delicious flavor he's ever tasted. And who knows-- maybe I am. All I know for sure is that I've never felt pleasure like this before. I didn't even know this kind of sensation was possible. There have been hot flashes of lust that seize me in the moment, but all of those were quick, fleeting moments that disappeared just as quickly as they emerged. This is something entirely different. This is musical. This is magical. This is...

Almost over.

"Oh my... my goodness," I whimper, trembling as he licks my pussy harder and faster, lifting me up to brand new heights of pleasure. His tongue expertly toys with my clit until I'm on the edge, gripping the sheets tightly with my legs hooked over Ironside's shoulders.

I arch my back, pushing my pelvis up against his face. I rut against his sensuous lips and his perfect tongue, my whole body buzzing with it as I bounce higher and higher. Ironside shows no signs of giving up anytime soon. If anything, he pushes me harder the closer I get to the precipice. He isn't afraid to give me the full extent of his expertise. His tongue toys with my clit. His lips suckle and kiss my trembling folds.

"It feels so good," I whisper, feeling sweat bead around my temples.

"Mmm," he groans against my clit, giving me delicious little vibrations that drive me absolutely wild. "Give it up for me, baby. Let me taste that sweet honey," he purrs.

"I'm so close. Oh my gosh," I sigh.

With one more flick of his tongue, my whole pussy explodes. I cry out and shiver intensely, the bed shaking as I ride the wave of incredible pleasure straight to the top. All the way through, Ironside's arms hold me down, his lips kissing my thighs and my pulsating cunny. He holds me and caresses me until I come tumbling down from that highest high. I'm exhausted, my whole body spent. Ironside wipes his mouth and gives me a satisfied smirk as he moves up to lie down next to me. I snuggle up close to his chest and he rests his chin on the top of my head.

"Oh. I can't believe I just did that," I gasp as he pulls me close.

"You're alright. I got you," he murmurs into my ear.

"I'm not a virgin anymore," I whisper.

"Welcome to the real world, little girl. How do you feel?" he hisses.

"Overwhelmed," I confess. "And tired. So tired."

"Don't you worry about a thing, baby," he assures me with a kiss to the back of my head. "You're safe here with me. I will never hurt you, and I will never let anyone else hurt you either."

"I believe you," I mumble.

"I know you do," he purrs back.

As pleasure gives way to fatigue, I drift away and away, a smile of contentment on my lips. It's true. I believe every word he says. In fact, he may just be the only person in the whole world I really feel like I can trust. I can believe what he tells me. He's the hero who took me from the dark place and brought me into the light. He's the one who holds the key to my safety and to my pleasure. He is the way. He is everything to me. There's no safer place to fall asleep than here, in his arms.

I wake up with the same smile still lingering on my lips the following morning. As I swim through the sleepy fog to reality, my eyes flutter open and I stretch out like a cat in the bed. A yawn escapes my lips and I roll over in bed, already happy as I reach out for Ironside, longing to feel the reassurance of his hard body next to mine. But to my disappointment, he's already gotten up. I'm alone in the bed, sprawled out almost diagonally. I blush as I pull myself up into a sitting position and look around blearily. I didn't get a whole lot of sleep last night, but I got enough. And after that incredible, mind-blowing trick Ironside showed me, I went out like a light, sleeping heavy and hard. I feel more refreshed right now than I have ever before in my life, and I know it has nothing to do with this mattress. It's all him. All his magical handiwork and manhandling, the way he played my body like an instrument, stroking the most harmonious pleasures from my tired frame. I can still hardly believe it actually happened. There's a little part of me that feels worried, but mostly I just feel renewed. Like I've been sleeping for a thousand years. I have to blink my eyes over and over to make them focus in the dimness as I search for signs of where my handsome savior might have slipped away to.

When I look over to the door, I have to do a double take. Right in front of me is my mystery stranger, impressively doing curl ups on a metal bar artfully wedged into the doorway. His shirt is off, putting his incredible musculature on full display. I lick my lips as I watch his abs contract, his pecs twitching as he pulls himself up and curls back down. I find myself totally mesmerized by the power and control with which he holds his body. Every cell of his massive form works together in perfect rhythm to give him an edge over any competition. There is not a single shred of doubt in my mind that this man could jump higher, run faster and farther, and work harder than any other man I have ever met. Truthfully, I hardly knew a lot of men growing up. My father makes sure to keep me isolated. But I'm not a total shut-in. I've been around... boys before.

But Ironside is no boy. No, he's all man. And that makes me feel like maybe I'm more than just a girl. Although, as soon as he turns those dark eyes on me, I feel small and fragile by comparison. He is the predator and I am his dainty prey. But as he jumps down from the pull-up bar and saunters over to sit down on the edge of the bed, glistening with sweat and glowing with heat, I remember that he is also my protector. The shepherd of my lonely flock.

He reaches out a warm hand and I lean my cheek into his palm, sighing happily. He strokes my cheek softly as he regards me, an almost paternal affection in his eyes.

"How are you feeling this morning, little one?" he asks me gruffly.

My cheeks burn pink as I avert my eyes, but he tilts my chin to make me look at him. He won't take nothing for an answer. His thumb traces over my bottom lip and I press a soft kiss against it, making a smile flicker on his handsome face for just one glorious moment.

"I feel good," I reply coyly.

"And about last night," he continues, staring into my eyes. "How do you feel?"

"Good," I answer again, blushing hotly.

I wish I could tell him what I really feel. I wish I could show him how thankful and awed I am. How enraptured by him I have become in so short a time. But all I can manage is that one word, regrettably weak to convey my true feelings.

"Good," he repeats, accepting my answer as satisfactory.

Then he stands up and offers me a hand. I gladly take it, letting him pull me out of bed and onto my feet. He looks me up and down, then hands me back my clothes. He watches me as I dutifully pull on my old, dirty clothes. I can't just walk around half-naked, obviously.

"We need to get you some new duds in town today," Ironside tells me matter-of-factly.

"What do you mean?" I ask.

"Your clothes. You need something better than that if you're going to ride with me, little girl," he informs me with a smirk.

Before I can fully react to his remark, I'm distracted by something else. My nose twitches and immediately my stomach starts to growl. I can smell salty, herby food somewhere nearby, and suddenly that's all I can think about. I look around with almost comical desperation, and Ironside laughs.

"Bones brought takeout breakfast. They're eating upstairs," he says.

I look at him with the round eyes of a wild animal.

"Can we?" I breathe.

"Yes. Of course. You need a little nutrition after last night," he says, putting an arm around my shoulders as he leads me out and up the stairs.

We walk into the bar area to see a group of somewhat familiar faces gathered around. Everyone seems to be in a lighthearted mood, joking around and sipping what smells to me like champagne and citrus. There are takeout boxes filled with containers emitting the most incredible smells I have ever encountered. I don't know if it's just the sheer high quality of the food itself or if I'm just so starved for real food that my senses are heightened.

"Well, good morning, strangers," says one of the men I saw playing cards last night.

"You prefer savory or sweet?" asks the one I recognize as Bones.

"Oh, I could never choose," I murmur, feeling almost weak with hunger.

"I'll do savory. She'll do sweet. We'll share," Ironside decides for us.

I give him a thankful look. At this rate, I'm so hungry all that matters is that the food is edible. And as soon as the french toast, scrambled eggs, bacon, home fries, and biscuits touch my plate I basically inhale them. As we eat, the men chat and talk shop, mostly conversation that flies a little high over my head. Besides, I'm too distracted by the food and the handsome company to really care. I do manage to weave my way in and out of the conversation now and again once I've eaten enough to feel almost back to normal. We joke about the weather, the food, how we all slept the night before-- it's oddly domestic. They all get along like family or close friends, and that makes it easier for me to relax a little and even start to feel at home.

By the time we're done with breakfast and heading down to the room to tidy up and get ready for the day, I feel a little attached to the group. Gone is my fear and unease from yesterday. In the light of day, they all just seem like good people. And lately, I've been having a hard time finding good people.

And if this group is good, then Ironside is the best of the best. We climb onto his motorcycle together and putter off down the highway toward the small town nearby. It's a glorious sunny day and the wind whipping through my hair makes me grin like a fool. I rest my cheek against my hero's powerful back and keep my arms happily wrapped around his waist all the way into town. It's closer to a village than a city, with a small downtown area steeped in rich history and colonial architecture. Wyoming is a fairly threadbare state, population-wise, and this town certainly reflects that. Still, there are a few clothing shops we spend time inside, shopping around and trying on clothes. Well, more specifically, me trying on clothes that he picks out for me. The shopkeepers gush about how pretty I look, but it's when they step away and leave me alone with Ironside that I truly feel beautiful. He compliments and encourages me, even when I feel a little silly. He convinces me that I am, in fact, desirable and worthy just the way I am.

I love the way he watches me, pride apparent in his eyes. He spends money like it means nothing at all, buying me anything and everything I try on and love. And throughout the whole excursion, I notice him looking out for me. He is constantly checking windows and keeping an eye trained on the entrances and exits of each business. On the street, he walks me on the inside of the sidewalk, subtly shielding me with his massive body as we walk around, hand-in-hand. He redirects between shops to throw off any trail. He ducks into alleyways and checks for tailing cars here and there. I have never felt so doted upon, so safe and secure.

It's nearing four in the afternoon when we finally pull back up to the clubhouse. As we slide off the bike and Ironside leads me back into the building, he has a smile on his face.

"You know, I haven't had fun like that without the aid of bourbon or a fight in a long time," he tells me.

"Glad to be of service," I toss back playfully.

We get back to the room and he shuts the door as I adoringly lay out each new item of clothing on the bed so I can see it all and make a choice. He saunters up behind me, helping me unzip myself and try on new digs. He stands back and watches me as I pull on a floaty pink dress. He bites his lip and shakes his head, looking at me like I'm made of pure sugar.

As he comes over to sit on the bed, I toy with the idea of toying with him. But before I even get a chance to push my luck, he pulls me into his lap, feeling me all over with those masterful hands. He leans in and kisses me hard on the neck, giving me goosebumps and making me shiver in his embrace.

"Oh goodness," I breathe. "I've wanted you to do that all day long."

"Mhm, baby. I know," he purrs, grazing his teeth along my neck. "But it's a hard road going down with you, little girl. A hard road."

IRONSIDE

$\mathcal{I}$ told myself I wouldn't. I've done that plenty of times in my life, and I always mean it. But Justine whittles me down like nobody else has ever been able to, and something about her is so magnetic that I can't say know, even if all my better judgment is telling me not to.

But the warm figure sitting on my lap is just too much to resist. Worse, now she knows it--she can feel the thick trunk between my legs now, and she knows just how hard it is. She feels just how much it can swell up for her, and the way she runs her hands down my thick jeans tells me she's still craving this as much as she was last night.

"I don't care if it's not easy," she hisses, pushing her ass back against me and grinding against my cock. "Maybe I want it hard."

I grin and let out a soft, low chuckle that gives

her goosebumps. Her small frame is so soft and delicate that I feel like I could break her if I'm not careful. The poor thing is giving me a look that tells me she wants to be broken, but she doesn't know what she's asking for.

"You're persistent," I growl, "I'll give you that."

"I need this, Ironside," she whimpers as I squeeze her hips. "I've never felt safe with anyone like I feel safe with you. I want to be good to you like you've been good to me."

The girl knew what she was about, that was for sure. And it was hard to fault her for her feelings, all things considered. She needs someone strong in her life to have her back, and she's dead-set on that person being me...in more ways I was expecting.

I can't deny my feelings anymore, not when a person like Justine is opening up to me and showing me an innocence I long since thought I'd forgotten. It hit me just then. Maybe it was something more than just the spirited personality I was really starting to like about her. I see something in her that isn't tainted the way I am.

There's something so comforting about that, that it warms every nerve in my body from my heart to the tip of my cock. My hands slide up her legs, and I feel painfully sinful with every inch that they grope. She lets out a soft breath and shivers as my hands touch her.

"I want this off," I growl into her ear. "Take this off. All of it."

She nods her head softly and slowly strips her clothes off in my lap, sliding as much of it off as she can before I twist her body around to help her out of the rest, until she's left in nothing but her underwear. She looks down at herself as I let her topple over onto the bed, and she blushes, looking up at me as I kneel on the edge.

"I said *all* of it," I growl as I pull my shirt off and toss it aside.

The blush on her face grows, and those quick, curious eyes of hers count my abs and drink in the broad, tattooed frame before her. Her eyes linger on the side where I took a frag grenade so many years ago, scars still visible under the tattooed words "IRONCLAD."

She sits up on her knees and walks forward on them to me, looking at the scars and bringing her fingers to them. She looks up at me with the same look I saw when she cleaned my wounds. She's a caring soul, and I can tell she wants to find the pain in me to ease it. But she doesn't deserve to get thrust into cold reality that jarringly.

I put one hand over hers and run my fingers through her hair with the other. "Old wounds," I say. "Long since healed."

"It doesn't look like it," she says softly.

I grin.

"Brat," I say, tightening my grip on her hair and making her mouth fall open. "For someone on the run, you stick your nose where it doesn't belong too much."

"I know," she admits bashfully, bringing her fingertips to my waist and tracing along my belt. "Like I said...I'm not exactly a stranger to discipline."

Her inexperienced, adorably clumsy words still thrill me to the core, and my every instinct knows with utter certainty what I need to do--what I *have* to. My fingers tighten into a fist in her hair, and I loom over her, reaching around her back to the clasp of her bra.

"You sound like you're looking for punishment," I growl with a low chuckle as I unhook her bra.

"That's up to you," she says in a brazen challenge.

I slide her bra off her arms and push her back onto the pillows, swiping my tongue over my lips at the sight of her exposed breasts. She squirms back with wide eyes as I advance on her and seize her underwear, hooking my fingers under the waist and slipping them off easily. She's so suddenly naked before me that even she's surprised, and the strawberry-pink blush in her cheeks makes my cock feel tighter than it ever has.

She puts her legs together and writhes with a soft gasp as I open my belt and unbutton my pants. Her eyes are fixed on the taut vee that points to my crotch as I slide the tattered denim down. I reach into my pants and take a large handful of my thick shaft and heavy balls, and when I let them spill out, Justine's mouth falls open.

I wrap my hand around my cock and give it a few good strokes, looking thoughtfully down at her with narrowed eyes that make her shiver and grasp the sheets.

"I want to take you," I say, "but I don't know if you deserve it."

"I've been good!" she protests, suddenly looking alarmed. "Please, I'll do anything!"

"I'm not so sure," I growl, sliding my hands between her legs and prying them apart with such ease that it's almost a joke.

Her wet pussy is already glistening, and my harsh gaze turns on her again.

"You've been thinking dirty thoughts," I point out, casually reaching forward and sliding a finger into her pussy.

Immediately, her back arches, and she gasps at the feeling of my thick finger pushing through those soft lower lips. I reach forward with my other hand and grope one of her breasts while a second finger joins the first, and no matter how hard she tries to close her legs, she's completely in my power.

"You're already so wet down here," I say with an almost condescending chuckle. "You really can't help yourself, can you?"

"I can't," she confesses in a pouting whine, hips

trying to twist, but my fingers curl in on her pussy and stroke away with a steady rhythm. "I need you. I need this--I want to feel you in me. No condom, just you."

"You're not talking like a good girl at all," my deep, husky voice rumbles as I feel her try to push her hips up into my hand's steady pace.

"I can be one," she urges me as I push her closer and closer to orgasm. "I can show you, I could-" A squeaky gasp cuts her off as her face flushes and her orgasm ripples through her body.

My hand feels how wet and ready she is, and I slide my fingers out and into my mouth to clean off. She watches me in vanquished awe--and I haven't even gotten started.

"I think I'll decide that," I say as I drape her legs one by one over my shoulders, pushing her backward and looming over her on my knees. "After I make you mine."

I push the tip of my bulging cock into the lips of her wet, slick pussy, and it slides in as if the two were made for each other. She lets out a sharp gasp, grasping the sheets at the sight of my pillar. I start to rock forward, slow but unstoppable, and I'm not cutting her any slack. If she wants to feel what it's like being with me, I'll let her *feel* it.

My shaft thrusts deeper into her, and the further I go, the more careful I get. Her eyes have been locked on my spear as it works its way further into her lips, and the satisfaction on her face from being filled up by me, inch by inch, is more soothing and energizing than anything I've ever tasted.

"At some point," I say, "you're going to feel a pinch. Don't panic. It's natural, and it only happens once."

"I'm not afraid," she says, nodding.

"Are you sure you want me to be the one to do that?" I say, my voice growing darker. "You can't take that back."

"I told you," she says, looking up at me with defiance through those desperate eyes. "I'm not afraid."

The spirit in this girl fills me with the same fire, and my cock stiffens even harder within her. She notices, and she pushes her hips up to feel more of me as I start to buck into her with building speed.

I've never felt anyone like this. Her pussy is tight and warm, and her lack of experience does nothing to make it worse. Every time I feel the slick, warm pressure of her pussy roll over the vein-ribbed length of my cock grinding against her insides, I feel a searing heat in me that's desperate to get out.

My heavy, virile balls want to release inside her. The heady scent of her in the air gives me the urge to rut into her like we're breeding. My hips start picking up the pace, and I grip her hips to buck into her deeper and harder than ever and feel her whole body tighten at once as an orgasm wracks her body...

...and she suddenly lets out a sharp whimper of

pain when my cock pierces her hymen, and the sheets tighten in her fists, but I lean forward and press a comforting kiss to her lips to soothe her. "It's okay, it's okay," I growl in a soothing voice like distant thunder. "I've got you."

I pepper her face in kisses, from her cheek down to her neck, and I slow my pace almost to a stop while I gauge whether she's in much pain. Her face was twisted up at first, but with each kiss and stroke, it seems to melt away little by little. She cracks her eyes open and looks at me with a hazy smile that makes my heart do a somersault, and I can't help but smile back.

"How do you feel?" I ask in a dark rumble of a voice.

"Better," she whispers. "That wasn't as bad as I thought. Thank you," she adds with a blush that only grows as I push myself deep into her.

I kiss her on the lips one last time before standing back up on my knees.

And now that she's broken in, I don't have to hold back anymore.

My comforting voice gives way to the husky grunting of a fierce rut as I pick my pace up again. I start pounding into her harder, feeling my heavy balls hit her ass as I claim the girl on her back in front of me. She's so goddamn wet that I can hear each time my cock plows through her, pulsing and feeling her natural rhythms to sync up with her pace perfectly.

The taut pressure in my cock builds so strongly that I feel like I'm going to burst or overflow if I don't do something about it soon. Even though I have more age and experience than her, she makes me feel like I've never felt before. I've never *craved* to release inside someone like this.

I want her to come with me, so I'm patient--I watch how she twists and sighs when I'm at this angle or that, feeling out her body and getting to know it. She might not even know it herself, for all I know. But when I find that sweet spot, I hammer it hard, grinding against it with my bulging crown as it gets bathed in her honey. Once I'm there, it doesn't take long for her to suck in a sharp breath through her teeth and run her nails down my sides as an orgasm crashes through her.

My balls tighten, and I groan as a thick shot of heavy seed erupts from my cock and plasters the inside of her pussy. Pulse after pulse, I pump everything I've got into her, utterly spilling myself into her untouched, fertile pussy. Her face is burning and glistening, and as the last few pulses of seed spurt from me, I lean forward to caress her body and kiss that needy mouth.

She moans into the kiss as our tongues brush together, and I feel closer than ever to this girl I only met yesterday. My cock is still stiff in her, and I feel like I could stay forever. When we finally break the kiss, she's glowing, and her innocent gaze looks up at me in awed reverence.

"How do you feel now?" I ask softly, stroking her hair.

"Safe," she murmurs, beaming up at me.

I slowly slide out of her and grab a towel nearby to clean up before I slide into bed against her and hold her close, listening to her murmur as she melts into my rough, hardened body.

"I meant what I said earlier," she whispers to me through the calm silence. "About how you make me feel. I can't explain it. I know you think I'm naive, but I know what I see in you."

I open my mouth to answer, but I'm interrupted by the sound of a loud and sudden banging on the door that makes Justine jump in my arms. I squeeze her shoulder and cover her in the blanket before standing up and pulling my pants up and closed.

"This had better be important," I mutter to myself before yanking the door open just enough to stick my head out.

I'm greeted by the sight of Skid, one of our members, looking at me slack-jawed and pointing up the stairs, where I hear commotion.

"Ironside, we've got a situation, it's an emergency," he says urgently. "One of Diesel's officers just pulled up outside."

I blink in disbelief. "*What?*"

"Yeah," he says, and I can tell when Skid isn't kidding around. "And you're never gonna believe this: he wants out."

~

A minute later, I throw the front doors open and stride outside, fully dressed and wearing my kutte as the afternoon sun casts an orange light on the scene in front of the bar. Against my will, of course, Justine is already at the nearest open window, watching with wide eyes as I approach.

Bones and Big Daddy both have shotguns trained on a tall man straddling his bike, and Breaker stands between them, arms crossed, staring the man down before turning his head to look at me. He gives a nod as I approach.

"Welcome to the party," he says. "Looks like we've got ourselves a wannabe turncoat."

"No shit?" I say, narrowing my eyes at the man.

He's broad-shouldered and built strong and lean. He's a few years younger than me, and he looks like he knows how to throw his weight in a fight. His eyes show their tension even though he's keeping a mild face, hands raised and fingers splayed.

"Again, guys, you've literally got me at gunpoint," the turncoat says, trying to sound affable. "The reinforcements are starting to be a little much."

"Don't make me come over there and gag you," Big Daddy growls. "It's been a slow day, I don't need much of an excuse."

"What's your name?" I ask the guy, brow furrowed.

"Tank," he grunts, and I notice the kutte hanging on his handlebars.

"And what's that?" I ask, pointing to Diesel's MC colors.

"Like I was tellin' your friend here," he says, nodding to Breaker, "that's my peace offering. I'm Diesel's enforcer, and I'm here to talk, since putting that fucker in the ground seems to be a, uh, mutual interest of ours," he says, gesturing between us with a still-raised hand.

"That why you're here?" Breaker asks. "To betray a man who trusts you?"

"Yup," he says bluntly. "Put a knife and his back and twist until I don't have to twist no more."

"This is obviously a trap," Bones says, glancing back at us. "Right? I mean, come on."

"Mighty strong words for Diesel's trusted man," Breaker points out, nodding. "Don't know if I can trust a traitor. But hey, a dead Buzzsaw is better than nothing."

"Why'd you change your mind so quick?" I ask Tank, crossing my arms.

He gives a snort of a laugh. "Trusted man my ass. I'm the fucker's cousin."

Our eyebrows collectively go up in surprise.

"I signed up with him when I heard he was running an MC since I had nowhere else to go," he says with a shrug of his shoulders. "I'd just been discharged, and we both rode, so it sounded good to me. He kept me at a distance, tried to keep me in the dark about what was going on with the girls."

"So you *were* involved in that?" Breaker says as Bones and Big Daddy steady their aims again.

"Shit, I slowed his operation down any way I could," he growls, smile fading. "Trucks breaking down, people getting tipped off, I was careful, but I knew he'd have me dead before sundown if I just tried to bail on the whole thing. So I did what I could from the inside, and now I want out," he says, looking at each of us pointedly. "I've got the contacts to prove it, too."

"Oh, don't worry about that," Breaker says with an ominous smile. "We'll get the truth out of you, if it's there. Get him inside," Breaker orders, and the two gunmen lower their weapons to approach Tank and pull him off the bike.

"Easy, bud," he grunts at Bones, who has him by the wrists. "If I came here looking for a fight, you'd know.

The guys lead him inside, and I bring up the rear. I catch Justine's pale face in the window as she watches the proceedings, and I feel a twinge of guilt that she's being exposed to something as crude as this. Her eyes follow us all the way to the stairs and down them into the clubhouse proper, as Breaker looks over his shoulder at me with a wicked smile.

"Old Ironside here has military experience too," he says to Tank. "I hear he's a specialist at getting people like you to sing for us."

Even though I feel Justine's eyes on my back, I need to put the group's needs first and keep this stranger on his toes. I reach behind me and unsheathe my combat knife, pretending I can't hear Justine's soft, troubled gasp. I look over my shoulder to see her disappearing into my room, and I frown.

The guys lead Tank into our meeting room, but I pause by one of the members lounging in the downstairs seats, watching us.

"Make sure the girl doesn't leave the building," I order him. "She can wander, but she stays in these walls until we know it's safe."

"You got it, boss," the biker says as I stride into the room and see Tank's reflection in my knife before I let the door swing behind me.

JUSTINE

I should be terrified to the core. I should be absolutely quaking as I sit here frozen in place, perched on the edge of the bed, my eyes trained on the door. How could I ever have been so foolish as to think the rough-edged man who saved me could be a real prince charming? How could I have lulled myself into such a false sense of safety? I heard the way those men yell at each other, how they hurled out that threat about Ironside pulling a mean interrogation if he needed to. It's such a stark contrast to the lovely, attentive, compassionate man who has shown me little else but pure kindness and tolerance despite the tangled-up mess we have fallen into together. I sit here, gently swinging my legs and rocking back and forth, as I so often do when faced with a complex conundrum. And what I saw out there looked just like a scene from one of those myriad gangbanger movies my parents would never have allowed to touch our television set back home. But still, there have been times when I managed to sneak down to the den after all my family members are asleep, so I could curl up on the sofa and watch crime shows on mute, my eyes squinting to follow the subtitles just so I'd have some faint idea of what was going on. Through these private, secret viewings, I gleaned what it means to be in an interrogation room, to have that bright fluorescent light beaming painfully into your eyes while you grapple with the truth and the lies that brought you there in the first place. Or at least that's how my admittedly active imagination fills in the scene.

And it certainly didn't seem like Ironside or any of the others were joking around out there. They were serious. They meant business when they dragged that big new guy into the clubhouse. I have no doubt about the fact that Ironside is capable of intimidation and interrogation tactics. Although he has been overwhelmingly patient and gentle with me, I can sense the urgency and the determination crackling like electricity just beneath the surface. He's a powerful man with formidable skills, and I should be very, very afraid of him. And in some ways, I am. He strikes an impressive figure. But underneath my fear is something even more powerful than anything else I have ever felt before: affection. Closeness. A longing to be intimate, not just physically, but emotionally and spiritually, with the man who could snap me in half without breaking a sweat. Something about him just draws me right in. He makes me weak and vulnerable at the same time that he makes me feel empowered. I am reminded suddenly of the things I learned in school about the moon and her light. The sun is the true powerhouse producing its own heat and light, but the moon can only glow when she shares that light with the sun. Perhaps that is not so far off from what I have been slowly building up with my mysterious savior. He is the sun, blazing red-hot and bright, and I am the moon, glowing stronger and more beautiful when he is standing behind me.

Suddenly, it feels like the bottoms of my feet are itchy. Longing to get moving, to get closer to the sun whose rays I miss like the morning misses the stars. I can't just sit here wasting time and twiddling my thumbs while something definitely interesting and potentially dangerous carries on just down the hall. I'm antsy, restless like a tumbleweed blowing across the dusty desert crust. I am compelled by curiosity to slide off the bed, pad softly across the room, and peek out into the hallway. Most of the doors are shut completely or left wide open, but there is one door down the hall which is only partly ajar, a tiny crack that gives out a flicker of light from within. I can hear several male voices communicating among each other, but most notably, Ironside's deep, sonorous rumble. I realize as I step along the hallway that they are all gathered in the meeting room. I slide like a shadow down the wall, close enough to flatten myself out but not close enough to brush against the wall and make a noise. I hope they can't hear my heart racing as I sidle up to the door. I hold my breath and strain my ears to listen.

The first voice I can isolate is Ironside's. To my relief, he sounds commanding but not cruel. His tone is even and calm as he asks questions. The voices sound tense, certainly, but not like there's any actual torture going on. Thank god. Yet. That is mildly comforting.

And when I hear the voice of the man called Tank, it becomes even clearer to me that this is not so much an interrogation as a discussion. He seems to be just as involved in the conversation as anyone else. Maybe more.

"Look, I didn't roll up here to start trouble with you all," Tank defends himself. "I don't have beef with you. It's Diesel I'm looking for."

"Well, then, you've come to the wrong place," interjects Bones. "Like we told you before: Diesel ain't here."

"If that's true, then there's something else I have to ask of you," says Tank.

"And what might that be?" growls Ironside. A shiver runs down my spine.

"Protection," Tank says flat out. "Protection from Diesel and his cohorts. Way I see it, the best way to do that and align myself against the bastard is to join you all."

"Join us, how?" Breaker asks warily.

"I want to be one of you. A Heartbreaker," Tank answers.

"Ha," one of the others scoffs.

"I'm serious," Tank asserts.

"Right, and what would you have to offer us?" asks the one I think is called Big Daddy.

"More than that," Ironside says. "How can we possibly trust you in the first place?"

"Good fucking question," Breaker grunts.

"Yeah, we have no reason to believe a word you say, kid," Big Daddy agrees.

I can hear a hint of smugness in his voice when Tank replies slowly, "Well, I just so happen to have some information that might make us bosom buddies if you just give me a chance to explain it to you."

"Great. Here's your chance," Ironside says imperiously. "Start talking."

"Alright, thank you! So, just for starters, I can give you the name of one of Diesel's most popular and successful clubs: Eden's Backdoor. A little on the nose, I know, but trust me when I tell you it's a fitting name. What's more: I know exactly how many men are guarding it. I know precisely how many girls they have working there right now," Tank reveals.

"Sure you do," Bones quips.

"Yeah, I think we're going to have to get that information confirmed for ourselves rather than trusting your best guess," Breaker insists.

"It's not a guess. It's a fact," Tank growls. "Why are you all so resistant to the truth?"

"I don't know you, man. You haven't earned my trust. Your truth is no better than mine as far as I can tell," Big Daddy insinuates.

"I like to do my own research," Breaker adds.

"Ugh, you're wasting time!" Tank groans. "Just listen to me!"

"You know so much and yet you still couldn't figure out Diesel isn't here with us? Rolled up here guns-a-blazing, thinking you got it all figured out," Bones says. "Sounds fishy to me."

"Stop," Ironside interrupts firmly. "There's no need to confirm what Tank says. I already did. I scoped that place out: Eden's Backdoor. I suspected it was one of Diesel's locations back then, but I didn't have proof in hand at the time."

As I hear him say those heart-stopping words, I notice that if the door is just slightly more ajar, I could probably see into the room. My chest aches as

I hold my breath and slowly reach to nudge the door farther open with my thumb at my side. I'm peering over my shoulder, trying to bend ever so slightly around the molded cornice of the door frame to look into the room. I know it's a huge risk I am taking, but my curiosity burns inside of me like a bonfire, and I can no easier leave it alone than stop breathing. That has always been my detriment-- I have to fight for knowledge. I have to push out and out further into this wild world to fill in the gaping crevasses of things I don't understand. It's never enough for me to simply stand quietly by and eavesdrop with my ears. Of course, not. I have to see the scene unfolding with my own two eyes in order to be properly satisfied. It's to my detriment, I'm sure, but I can't resist. I have to look.

So I crack the door just marginally more open and slowly, silently turn to look into the room with one eye. As soon as my eye adjusts to the depth and distance, I notice a large table around which the men are seated. And at the far head of the table, facing my way directly, is Ironside. Instantly, I freeze up, terrified to breathe or move a muscle. He's not looking right at me, but he might as well be. I shrink back from the door slightly, but still give myself a tiny sliver to observe with my one eye open.

"So, then, you should know for a fact you can trust me! I have all the right information, I swear. I can give you numbers. I might even be able to give you some names if you let me think about it," Tank asserts.

"I don't know about this," Big Daddy grunts, sounding unconvinced.

"Yeah, me neither. I don't like it," says Bones, shaking his head. "Think about it, guys. It could all just be a setup."

"What the hell are you accusing me of now?" Tank snaps.

"You heard me," Bones hisses back.

"Now, Bones, hold up. If this was all a big setup, then they could have gone through a hell of a lot less trouble than sending this guy to spy on us," Breaker points out.

"Still, I don't think he's worth the risk to keep him around," Big Daddy insists.

"The risk? I'm offering you rewards! I'm an asset, can't you see?" Tank claims.

At just that moment, Ironside's eyes finally flick straight to me. My body stiffens up and my blood runs icy cold. I can feel my heart stuttering and tripping over itself as alarm bells sound off in my head. His gaze is only locked onto mine for a few seconds, but it might as well have been a few hours. The effect is the same. I'm stunned and startled and regretting my decision to rudely eavesdrop on business that has nothing to do with me.

I hear Ironside's voice strike up and I'm nearly dizzy with worry, thinking he's going to call me out. But then, he simply says, "We ought to send our new friend Tank back to Diesel to play the mole for our side. You know the deal. Feed us info on the down-low. Keep Diesel's suspicions off our backs."

"Now, wait just a minute," Big Daddy grumbles.

"I'm in! I'll take it!" Tank interjects enthusiastically.

"You're ballsy enough to do that? Really?" Bones scoffs.

"Hell yes. I want to take Diesel down by whatever means necessary, you understand?" Tank declares. "I'm not afraid to get my hands dirty."

"So, what's the plan, then?" Breaker asks.

Ironside answers coolly, "We send Tank back to Diesel with a good cover story to explain his absence. He falls back into ranks, works his way up through the bullshit to get there. To get close to Diesel. We stay in communication, but we make it as low-risk as possible. And then, when it comes time to strike, we'll set up something that'll hit Diesel. Hard."

"You think this guy can handle all that, Ironside?" Bones asks dubiously.

"What do you say, Tank?" Ironside puts to him.

"I say throw me in, coach," he agrees eagerly.

Great," Ironside says. I feel another shiver run

down my spine when I hear his chair legs scrape lightly across the floor, then his echoing footsteps as he stands up. Oh god. And when I hear the next words out of his mouth, I feel like I might collapse where I stand.

"Where you going, man?" Breaker asks him.

"I'm going to go deal with our little eavesdropper," Ironside growls.

I let out a tiny squeak of fear and go barreling down the hallway to the bedroom, my heart pounding away like crazy in my chest. It hurts to breathe, my whole body is in full-fledged panic mode. I can't help it-- the sound of a man coming after me, the growl of a man's voice as he accuses me, the rush of my own blood in my ears, the tears burning in my eyes-- it's all a reflex response to the sensation of being caught red-handed by a powerful man. My father instilled in me a kind of fear I still fall apart to face.

Before I can even get through the door, Ironside has caught up to me. I cry out in primal fear as his hands land on my shoulders. He spins me around and pins me against the wall inside the room, leaning in close so I can feel the angry heat radiating from him.

"What is the matter with you?" he snarls.

"Leave me alone! You're hurting me!" I whimper, trying to squirm away.

"I am not hurting you," he hisses, and he's right, I

realize. Even though he has me fully cornered, I'm not in any pain. His hands on my shoulders are soft, but firm... yet not painful. That almost makes me more upset.

"Let me go," I sniffle.

"Why do you want to go sniffing your little nose around in club business?" he accuses.

"I'm sorry," I sigh. "I just... I couldn't resist, okay? I'm all alone here and I don't have any clue what's going on because nobody will tell me anything and I--I just needed answers!"

"Answers to what?" he groans.

"Anything! Who you are, where you come from, what you're like-- I want to know everything because you're the only person who has shown me any hope and I just want to make sure that the man I'm counting on is, you know, on the right side!" I blurt out, blushing hotly.

"Goddamnit," he sighs, looking at me with what seems to be worry.

"I've never seen an interrogation in person before. And I wanted to know if it was true what I heard them say about your interrogation skills," I explain.

"And?" he asks. He sounds exasperated.

"You still seem like a good guy to me," I admit softly.

Ironside looks at me differently then. His black eyes soften. Grow warm. He reaches one immense hand to cup my cheek delicately. He says, "I think you could use a break from all this."

"What do you mean?" I ask, wide-eyed.

"Come on," he says, taking my hand. "I know the place."

The diner is virtually empty at this hour, except for the high school kids necking in the corner booth and the old trucker reading a mystery novel at the coffee counter. And then there's us: Ironside looking like a handsome stranger from the wrong side of the tracks and me, his innocent-faced sidekick. We lean in to eat burgers and fries, the two of us sharing one vanilla-chocolate swirl milkshake with two hot pink straws. I feel like we've stepped into the set of some old-fashioned, wholesome sitcom. But the man sitting across from me is more hardcore than family-friendly. Still, I can't deny that he's been oddly sweet to me.

"Tell me about yourself," he says. "How did you grow up?"

"Well, to make a long story short, I always followed the rules and look where it got me," I admit, realizing how very jaded I actually am. "I trusted my father to take care of me. To have my best interests in mind. But it turns out, he's only ever seen me as a piece of property. Just another potential dollar sign to cash in."

"I am sorry to hear that," he says meaningfully. "You deserve so much better."

"Thank you," I reply, picking at my fries.

"And you know, you don't have to do what they told you you're supposed to do. You have other options, little girl. You don't have to do what your Daddy says. You just have to do whatever is going to make you happy," Ironside assures me.

My heart flutters and a genuine smile hitches itself to my lips. I hadn't known just how badly I needed to hear those words from somebody. And thank god, it was him.

"So, little miss Justine," he says playfully, leaning in close with those black eyes blazing, "if you could look into the future and see your wildest dreams come true, what would you see?"

I giggle and blush, trying to wrack my brain for an answer. The truth is, I have hardly ever given myself a moment to think about the future. Well, other than the prescribed future my parents laid out for me. As I'm thinking it over, I realize I need to use the restroom.

"I'll be right back," I tell him, hopping up.

He lets me go, as the restroom is just several feet away, within eyesight of the table. I slip into the restroom and start doing my business, happily considering my future with an open mind-- until I hear something strange and unsettling outside the bathroom door.

There's a voice-- no, two voices. One of them is Ironside, the other sounds like the stiff, formulaic speech patterns of a rookie cop. And then I hear the cop say something that horrifies me to my core.

My name.

My full name.

"Justine Smith," the officer in front of me says.

My heart is racing, but my gaze up at the police officer's narrowed eyes looks like the picture of innocence as I keep my nerves under control. I'm used to keeping a clear head under pressure. This is dangerous, but if it were a lost cause, I'd be thinking about plan B already. This officer strode just after the waiter left the table, and now he's asking me about a missing person last seen heading in this direction.

"She's about 5'5", light red hair, nineteen years old," he goes on, giving me that stern, suspicious look I know all too well. "Sweet little slip of a thing, you wouldn't forget the sight of her around here," he adds with a chuckle.

Law enforcement tends to have a chip on its

shoulder about bikers, and to be fair, we give them plenty of reason to. And since even though the officer who strode in had almost definitely been given a description of a kidnapper that looks a lot like me...I need to watch my every word.

This is our territory. Even the police officers who aren't on the take know that fact and respect it. I've seen this officer's face before, but we've never met in person, so he doesn't know me. What he thinks of the kutte hanging on my shoulders is up in the air.

"Sounds like I wouldn't," I say with a gruff chuckle. "Take a seat, officer, tell me more. Maybe I can point you in the right direction."

The officer eyes me carefully for a few seconds, then his eyes pan down to the table. But the waiter had just come to collect our plates, and there's no evidence left at the table that I'm not alone.

Once again, luck pulls through for me.

"I'll stand," he says, still regarding me skeptically. "So you've never seen this woman at all? Not even at the bar where you fellas get together?" he asks.

"If she's nineteen," I say, "she wouldn't have been in our bar. Anyone at the station can back you up on that."

"Uh-huh?" he says, moving his jaw side to side with a stony expression.

"Mind if I write all that down?" I ask, reaching for the pen still sitting on the signed check for the bill. "I'll pass it along to our prez. We look out for our own in Crook County."

Sure enough, the officer tersely repeats his description of Justine, which I write down on the back of a clean napkin that I then hold up with a gruff smile before tucking it safely into a pocket. The officer watches all of this, looking like he's trying to decide whether I'm guilty and throwing him off-- which I absolutely am--or just fucking with him.

We kind of have a reputation for that, to put it lightly.

"If we get any eyes on her, we'll make sure you're the first to know. Any idea what the situation is? Is she a runaway? Any direction she's headed?"

"Came from up northeast, might be in the company of a biker," the cop says. "White male, thirties, tattoos-"

"You're gonna arrest a hell of a lot of bikers with that description, officer," the waiter says with a good natured smile as he busses the nearby table. The officer glares at him, but his gaze pans back to me judiciously.

"Your club has a reputation for keeping our girls safe," the officer says begrudgingly. "I hope you live up to your reputation. If you see something, call us," he says, scowling and heading out the door.

The waiter and I exchange a look, and I chuckle, shaking my head and hiding just how relieved I feel.

"Think he's a rookie," the waiter says as I stand

up and head to the bathroom to give Justine the coast-is-clear signal. "He'll get used to y'all."

"Don't mind us, Brent," I say, giving him a wave. "We know how to break 'em in."

I get to the door and knock on it with the back of my hand. "Justine," I whisper loudly to her through the door.

It cracks open slowly, and Justine's pale face pokes through and looks around before breathing a sigh of relief. I take her by the hand and lead her out as she looks up at me and takes a deep breath.

"Did I hear…?" she asks.

"You did," I say with a curt nod. "But I got it under control. We're out of the frying pan for now."

"Isn't the second part of that saying-"

"Yeah," I grunt, "I didn't say we were out of the fire yet."

"Are they looking for me?" she asks with a hard swallow. "What do we do? How do we get out of here?"

She stands closer to the little hallway leading to the bathrooms to stay out of sight of the parking lot, where the officer is hovering around his squad car on his radio. I watch him for a moment, then turn back to Justine and put my hands on her shoulders.

"He thinks we don't know each other," I say. "But if he's out looking for you, he has backup in town. If they have a biker fitting my description and a girl fitting your description together in their crosshairs, we can't be seen together."

"Do you mean we need to leave separately?" she asks, eyes widening.

"Not exactly," I say, glancing at the window briefly. "I need him to see me leaving alone, and you need to not be seen at all."

"How do we do that?"

"Do you remember the lawyer's office two lots down?" I ask, thinking for a moment.

"The one with the green sign? I remember," she says, nodding.

"Leave out the back, through the kitchens," I say, "and don't stop for anything. Pretend you belong there, like you know what you're doing and you know where you're heading."

"O-okay," she says, nodding hesitantly, and I squeeze her shoulders reassuringly.

"Stay behind the buildings and meet me behind that office. I'll bring the bike around and pick you up."

"Are you sure about this?" she asks, reaching up and taking my hands.

"I trust you," I say with a slow nod. "You can do this. I know you can."

She looks uncertain at first, but she finally takes a deep breath and nods. "Okay. Let's go before it's too late."

I lean in and give her a kiss on the lips before

looking to the cop's car. He has opened the front door and is sitting with one leg out, facing away from the diner--now's the only chance we might get.

"Go, straight for the kitchens and out the back," I say, turning her and letting her jet to the back doors, power-walking while smoothing her hair out and trying to compose a confident stride.

I watch her go until she's through the doors, and I then head out the front doors myself, dropping a $50 on the table for Brent as a thank-you for his discretion. It pays off to be regular and tip well.

The officer's eyes are on me almost as soon as I'm out the door, and I pretend not to be watching him as I make my leisurely way to my bike. When my ass hits the seat, I take out my phone to just as leisurely text Breaker that the boys in blue are eyeballing me, and that I might take the long way home.

That will tell Breaker all he needs to know to give me a hand, directly or indirectly. There's no way this officer is the only one prowling the town for Justine tonight.

I fire up the engine of my bike and pull out of the parking lot, giving the cop a nod as I go. I feel his eyes on me all the way down to the end of the block, where I turn the corner and vanish into the darkness of the night.

Immediately, I quiet my engine and circle back around through the businesses' back lots, rolling over cracked asphalt and cutting my headlights. In the flickering shadow of a floodlight, I see Justine step out from the side of a building, and I let out a relieved breath.

Before my bike has even stopped completely, she throws her arms around me and kisses me before she hops onto the back of my bike and hugs me from behind, not just holding on but pressing herself into my back and putting her head to it as I turn the bike around and roll out.

"You did great, baby," I tell her, reaching behind me to squeeze her thigh. "I knew you would. Surprised you didn't run for the cop while you had the chance."

"Who do you think I'd trust, you or some stranger?" she says without missing a beat, making my heart swell warmly more than she probably knows. "The cooks looked at me funny," she admits, "but I just kept my eyes on the back door, and I think they knew what I was doing but didn't mind."

"Our people are good people," I say proudly, and I pull out onto the street.

Sure enough, we aren't far away before I notice another squad car parked in an alley, sitting idle. I keep my headlights off and wait for another car to pass and take the light with it before crossing the road carefully and rolling through a small neighborhood where I know the police rarely come prowling when searching the highways.

"We'll take it slow and dark," I tell her as she

watches the various yards pass her by. "Breaker is probably hitting up our pocket-cop and getting him to thin out some of the squad cars looking for you.

Sure enough, while I'm at a stop behind an old shed on a street corner in the shadows, I watch a couple of police cruisers sail by away from the direction I'm heading--most likely to a false alarm conveniently on the other side of town.

I pull back out into the road, and I take off for the clubhouse, heart pounding as the dry air kisses our faces on the rest of the road back to our sanctuary.

When I finally lead Justine by the hand through the front doors of the bar and make a beeline for downstairs to get her out of sight, it truly does feel like coming back to the one sanctuary I have left on this earth. The bar has a handful of the usual members drinking and chatting happily, and after the tension outside, it's a warm and inviting welcome.

Hiding Justine away while I'm at it makes it all come together as something truly worth fighting for.

Once we're downstairs, where the bar's empty, I'm not two steps into the room before I swing Justine around to the wall and press a fierce kiss to her, pinning her down with my hips and grinding against her. She moans delightedly, pleasantly surprised and squirming against me immediately. If I'm feeling the adrenaline rush, I can only imagine how she feels.

A rebellious streak is one thing, but coming that close to capture again and evading the police in foot is another. I had faith in her, and I knew it wasn't ill placed. I trusted her not to run to the cops, and she had all the opportunity to. She must have known there's a chance that cop might *not* have turned her over to the wrong hands. But still, she stayed with me and followed my orders perfectly.

She really is a good girl, after all.

"I'm going to take you again, little girl," I growl into her ear. "I know what you need, and I'll give it to you. And you'll like it."

She barely has time to nod her head before I pick her up by the hips and throw her over my shoulder, clutching her like a prize as she squeals. I carry her back to my room and throw the door open, toss her onto the bed, and lock us inside with a hungry smile.

Her shoes hit the floor before I reach her, and I seize her pants to work them open and slide them off her legs, taking her underwear with it and gazing on her bare legs with a ravenous look in my eyes. I have to restrain myself from lunging for her right then, and instead, I stand up to my full height and pull my shirt off, dropping it to the floor and grabbing one of her ankles.

Her eyes are full of desire and unwavering from me. She drinks in every inch of me as I drag her close enough to pull her up and take her shirt off. Her hair feels soft against my hands as I unhook her bra, and she gently rests her head against my hard-ened abs as I bring my hands up to stroke her hair. She shrugs out of her bra while I hold her, feeling her warmth--as well as a kind of warmth within myself.

I've never felt such a protective instinct for someone like I do for Justine. And I'm a man who has always had that instinct. For her though, it feels like a magnetic pull I can't explain, and it makes me want to spend every second I've got touching her. I hold her hair tight and gently pull it back to make her look up at me, and I take her chin in my hand to stroke her lip with my thumb.

"You weren't made for this life," I say to her. "You shouldn't have to be doing this."

"It doesn't feel normal," she say, her eyes looking pensive, "but...is it...bad if I kind of like it?"

"Like it?" I say, chuckling. "You like riding, don't you?"

"Not just that," she says, uncertain. "I mean, that *is* nice. But I just never knew how riding would...feel? I don't know what I'm talking about."

"It's a rush," I say, grinning. "It's freedom. You can hold your own destiny in your hands on a good bike. There's a reason people join MCs. This is how we live," I say, squeezing her gently. "And it's not for everyone."

"Do you think it could be for me?" she asks boldly.

She wants me to call her naive again and get me to push back, and knowing that makes me grin. I push her back onto the bed, and she giggles, recoiling while I strip out of my pants and throw them aside before pouncing the bed.

I grab her by the ankles again and drag her toward me, and I start kissing my way up her sensitive inner thighs. My stubble brushes against the thin skin and tickles her, but when she starts to squirm and writhe away, I take her by the hips and hold her down.

I bring my mouth up to her firm, round breast and press a kiss to it. She shivers before I let my tongue wash over it and feel the stiffening nipple. I swirl my tongue slowly and tease it hard second by second. The sound of her moaning and sighing spurs me on, and my heart pounds and makes my naked body glisten in the dim light.

When I've had my fill of teasing her sensitive bud between my teeth, I tear myself away from her while still holding onto her, reaching for my phone on the nightstand and pulling up my music. I'm not planning to keep quiet, and if she wants to get excited about riding, she might as well get used to our music.

She blushes and laughs at the harsh rock that plays, and I grin before parting her legs with a hungry smile and grabbing her hips. I gruffly pull her pussy toward me like a meal I'm about to sink my teeth into, and when I let my tongue out, it tastes just as satisfying.

She's so wet for me already, and she has a lot to offer. I taste her honey over and over, moving my tongue side to side over her clit and swirling it in small circles with every new gasp I tease out of her. I feel lost in her, bare thighs grinding against my face while I lick her pussy clean. As my tongue dives into her, I feel her skin brushing against my stubble and giving her goosebumps.

We can't get enough of each other's bodies. It's intoxicating to me, and we're barely even able to talk. It doesn't take long for me to feel the need to be inside her, but I take my time with her, diving my tongue into her and dragging it out slowly between relentless rounds of tormenting the clit. Even my sharp teeth scrape against the tortured nub, and her scent is heady in the air as she finally plunges her hands through my hair and holds on.

She tries to cry out, but her voice cracks into a squeak as honey floods my face. I take in every drop, squeezing her in a soothing, approving reward as my mouth guides her through the orgasm. I want to spoil her while she's in my grasp, and if that means losing myself between her legs all night, I'll gladly do it.

She trusts me, and I'm going to deliver...and pray I'm not making a mistake by dragging her into all this.

JUSTINE

I am in heaven.

My whole body tingles and sparks with the electricity flowing through me like a bolt of bright white lightning. Ironside is between my thighs, drinking me up, nudging me to new heights of incredible pleasure. I have never felt like this before, not even in those forbidden fantasies my mind cooks up for me when I dream sometimes. I used to wake up sweaty and wracked with guilt, slick between my legs and confused as to how it happened. I guess all those years of repression and denial had to find an outlet somehow, and if I couldn't pursue my own pleasure in my waking hours, then at night my desires would creep back into bed with me. Those nights were always followed by a morning of deep shame and self-reflection. I used to think people could read it on my face, like there was a scarlet letter burned into my forehead to broadcast to the whole damn world what a slut I was.

Now, though, I am just finally starting to unfurl myself, and it has everything to do with Ironside. When he touches me, those long-repressed little fires flicker back to life. My body becomes a map of bonfires, all burning in adoration and awe of this mysterious man. I don't understand it, but somehow he manages to know exactly what I need, anticipating my every whim before it even occurs to me. He can not only read my mind, it seems like he can predict it. I am fully convinced that there's some kind of sorcery dispensed through his touch, his fingertips and his masterful tongue. Every little caress sends me careening into space, my body so overwhelmed and overstimulated that it makes my eyes water. He's devouring me once again, nibbling and suckling my clit as I spasm all over with delight. His tongue washes its way down my trembling flower, exploring every petal like it's something brand new and utterly divine to the taste. He laps me up with vigor, driven by a possessive need to claim me and make me his own. It feels so damn good that I don't intend to tell him yet that he's already won me over. He's already got me wrapped up around his finger like a pretty little ribbon.

"You taste so damn good, little girl," he purrs, taking a moment to glance up at me.

His handsome face is perfectly framed by my hips and thighs, a flawless fleshy portrait that stirs my heart. His lips are shiny with the slick of my honey, his square jaw and chin brushed pink by friction. I reach down to tangled my fingertips in his tousled hair, moaning as I guide him back down to my cunny. He dives down eagerly, flicking his tongue around my tingling clit. The tension is so powerful it almost burns. He's found the mystical root of my pleasure and he lays it bare, stroking without hesitation and soaking up my juices as I helplessly come over and over, gushing all over his face. He laughs softly and I can tell he's proud of himself. But when he looks up at me with those dark eyes hooded and full of fire, I can tell that he's proud of me, too. He knows how hard it's been for me to loosen up and give myself over to him, to fully lose myself in the crashing waves of climax. For once, I am not allowing my self-conscious worries to rise up and quash my pleasure. This time, I am giving up and giving in. I'm learning that I don't have to feel guilty about wanting what I want. I don't have to beat myself up for getting it.

I can feel good during and after. I can skip the shame and just embrace pleasure. I can't believe I ever wasted my time and energy on feeling bad about feeling good. I suppose that's the danger of living life entirely within the narrow lines of a sheltered existence. I never colored outside the lines. I never experimented beyond what I thought might still be forgivable on the scale of sins. I was so afraid of being stuck there, of letting my desires hang so heavily on my shoulders that they anchor me to damnation. Now, I don't care about damnation. As far as I'm concerned, there is no heaven without Ironside in it. He's the sign that all is well. He is the earthbound angel who has come here to teach me to feel at home in my body. It has always felt like someone else's property, like I'm just renting this form rather than owning it myself. My father must have really messed me up, I guess. I let him and his evil intentions possess and push me away from knowing my own heart. He's kept me at a distance, detached from my body. I guess that made it easier for him to sell it. But I own myself now. Or maybe Ironside does. Either way, I'm in safer hands than I ever was before.

It's kind of funny-- on the outside, my home growing up must have looked like the most perfect environment. Respectable, church-going parents. A sterile, tidy home. A healthy amount of responsibility and damn near constant supervision. But in reality, it was a den of vipers. I was always being watched, and yet also ignored. I had a lot to answer to but no right to ask my own questions. At least, that's the way I was taught. To repress my questions. To clamp down on my desires. My daddy may have raised a good girl, but there's always been a naughty girl underneath that facade, just waiting for the opportunity to burst free of her cage, almost spring-loaded and ready to go at the drop of a hat. It's crazy that it's taken extraordinary circumstances to get me here, but now that I know how good it feels, I don't plan to let it go anytime soon. I will drink as much pleasure from this unpredictable life as I can, and I know for a fact Ironside will help me do that.

He flicks his tongue over my clit again and I arch my back, tilting my head and letting my eyelids flutter shut. A wave of pleasure rolls up through my body and my hands grasp at the sheets. I curl my legs over his broad, powerful shoulders and work my hips, rubbing myself against his smooth, slick tongue. I can't hold back the moan that falls from my lips as he draws a tight circular motion around my clit and downward. His tongue plunges in and out of my pussy, playing with the sensitive band of nerves around my pulsing slit. I can't help but clutch at his hair, grasping for purchase as he devours me greedily. I don't know what it is about this man, but he seems completely unfazed by how many times I have already gushed all over his face. He doesn't care that I'm nearly oblivious with pleasure and overstimulation. He gives me so much intense attention that I'm almost shying away from it, but I know that's pointless. Ironside wants me to feel good, and he's going to keep me here as long as he can.

I can't believe how quickly I have adjusted to suit

him. Growing up, I always expected to marry an innocent man, a man who is on the same page as me sexually. I used to think that was the right way, that my equally sheltered husband and I would have to figure out how our bodies ticked together, slowly. But Ironside needs no reeducation. He knows exactly what he's doing, and that only makes it easier for me to relax. I know I am not only completely safe when he's here, but I know my pleasure in good hands. He's a master with his tongue and his hands feel like magic on my body. He's an expert in pleasure, and I am more than happy to be his willing pupil in the ways of sex and love. A part of me still wonders if I should fear him. He lives a wild, rollicking life, the kind of living that would have seemed too cinematic to be real in my mind growing up. Ironside is like a movie character who stepped out of the screen and into my world. I am continually amazed to be sharing the same space with him. We are a strange combination of traits, I know. And yet we fit like two locking pieces of machinery. Stronger together. An unstoppable force.

As I shudder and clench through yet another orgasm-- I've lost count at this point-- I look down at the mysterious man between my thighs and I pool together the strength to ask for something I never would have given breath to before Ironside opened up my eyes.

"I want to taste you," I tell him, with more clarity

and confidence than I'm used to hearing in my own voice. Ironside looks up at me, seeming impressed.

"Look at you making demands," he growls. "You want to taste me, little girl? You know what you're asking for?"

I nod, my heart thumping like crazy.

"Yes. Please," I murmur softly.

"Ask and you shall receive," he replies.

I watch with reverence as he moves up and slips off the bed for a moment to take off his pants and shirt. I feel the breath catch in my throat as I watch him, my eyes drinking in his rippling muscles and hard, raw strength. I can feel him nearly glowing with need. I'm impatient to give him the release he so badly craves. My eyes are locked into him as he moves up to the edge of the bed, one hand slowly stroking his massive cock. My mouth waters to feel him stretching my cheeks and pushing down my throat. I need this just as desperately as he does. He snaps his fingers, wordlessly calling me over to him. I come over to him on my hands and knees, eyes wide and mouth slightly parted.

He looms over me tall and imposing as I slowly bend to give the swollen head of his shaft an exploratory flick of my tongue. I'm immediately aroused by the taste of salty precome beaded at the tip. I moan involuntarily and wrap a small hand around his thick length, starting to lightly stroke up and down while I lean in to pull the engorged head into my warm, wet mouth. God, it feels good. The weight of his cock pressing into my mouth and back toward my throat. He twitches slightly in my mouth and I can feel a guttural groan of pleasure roll through body, nearly vibrating on my tongue. I suck in my cheeks and swallow, increasing the pressure around his shaft as I start bobbing up and down. His cock twinges in my mouth and it's all I can do to keep from moaning. Making him feel good makes me feel good. I love knowing that a girl like me has the capacity to satisfy a man like Ironside. His thickness stretches my cheeks and makes my face ache in the most delightful way. I'm in pure heaven right now, eagerly sucking him off and swallowing down every bitter drop. I can feel him starting to lose his control as a result of my hard work and I want it desperately. I long to taste his climax, to feel him shudder and release down my throat. I feel confident that if I just keep going like this I'll get him there. But to my dismay, he gently pushes back on my shoulders to stop me before he totally loses it. His cock slides out of my mouth with a slick, resounding pop and I pout up at him, awaiting his next move. He regards me with a predatory smugness that gives me shivers and turns me on at the same time.

"Lie back for me, sweetheart, and spread those legs," he purrs.

I do as I'm told. No hesitation. I flop back on the sheets and scoot up to rest my head on a pillow, watching with held breath as Ironside slinks up to me. Every cell in my body is ringing and thrumming with anticipation. I know what is to come, and I am more than ready to meet it. His cock twitches and bounces in the free air as he moves to straddle me. He grabs my legs and wraps them around his waist, lining up the head of his massive cock to my clit and giving it a slow, teasing circular rub. I tremble and bite my lip, rolling my hips to meet him.

"You're playing with me," I murmur.

"Yes, I am. I want you good and desperate, little girl," he growls. "I want you to beg."

Oh yes. Gladly.

"Please, Ironside, please fuck me," I whimper. I'm surprised to hear such a dirty word come from my own voice, and judging by the look on his face, Ironside wasn't expecting that either. But he looks down at me almost proudly.

"Good girl. That is exactly what I like to hear," he grunts.

I tremble while he lines up his cock against my slick cunny, spreading the petals of my flower to get ready access. I can hardly remember to breathe. I know what's to come and I am anxious for it. Ironside teases me with his cock a little more, and then promptly slides inside of me in one smooth, fluid movement. I cry out, clenching my legs around him as the thick head of his shaft knocks against my g-spot deep inside. White-hot pleasure smacks me across the face like a brick, my cunny aching and twitching around his thickness. He begins to slowly work his way out and then spears back into me hard, hitting and stimulating every trembling nerve and muscle on the way. He rears back and slams into me, my slick juices keeping us both perfectly lubricated. I can tell our extended foreplay session has ramped up his desires, because Ironside starts fucking me with abandon. He needs this just as badly as I do, and that realization turns me on like nothing else ever has before.

"You're so fucking tight for me, baby," he coos. "So perfect."

"It feels so good," I murmur breathlessly.

He pounds my pussy harder and faster, his hips pistoning back and forth as we both climb higher and higher together. We are both losing control, letting the waves of pleasure carry us without a single coherent thought. Everything is a bright flash of intense, overwhelming pleasure. Everything is tight and contracting and clenched for the great plunge. I can feel his body seizing up and going stiff just like mine. My muscles ache from tensing up so many times, but I know I'm going to feel incredible afterward. The soreness will be just another physical memento of this glorious time spent in the throes of bliss together.

"Give it to me," I whisper between gritted teeth. "Fill me up, Ironside. Please."

"You ready to take it, sweetheart? You sure?" he groans, teetering on the edge.

I nod vigorously, an act which makes my pleasure-addled mind feel dizzy. But it's all I can manage right now, so overwhelmed with the intensity of sensation as I hurtle toward another massive orgasm. Ironside pulls back and slams into me three more times, striking my g-spot without fail, until he grabs my hips with both hands, his fingertips digging in as he seizes up and comes inside me. I shudder through another climax of my own as I feel him emptying himself into my dripping cunny. He holds me in place and pumps me full of his come, both of us sighing and moaning one another's names in desperation. I stare up at him with awe. This man is dangerous. He could hurt me so easily. And yet, I am so irrevocably drawn to him. A part of me wishes I could have been arrange-married to him instead. Maybe then I would not have wanted to run away. Something tells me this is fate, that I would have found Ironside no matter which path I decided to take. He is my endgame. He is my destination, and as long as I am with him, I will be home.

He gently kisses me on the forehead before helping me up. Lovingly, he scoops me up into his arms and carries me damsel-style to the bathroom. I feel so safe and secure in his arms as he turns on the shower and the bathroom starts filling up with warm steam. We slip into the shower together, slowly rinsing off under the hot spray. I marvel at his glistening body, the bulging muscles, hard lines, and tattoos. His body is like a work of art, every inch of which I want to study and memorize. We wash each other's bodies, showing personal attention and caring for one another with warmth and softness. We stay quiet at first, but then he asks me a question out of the blue.

"What did you say the name of your hometown is?" he asks.

"Meadowville," I inform him. "Why? You're not actually thinking about going there to… to hurt my dad or anything, right?"

"Justine, I wasn't just blowing steam when I said I want to get you justice," he says rather cryptically. There's a serious look on his face.

"What do you mean?" I press him.

"I mean that we'll have some time to kill while Tank gets back to Diesel and settles into his position as a mole, and every minute we're waiting here, you're just a sitting duck," he says.

"Well, going back to Utah doesn't exactly sound like the safest option, either," I point out to him, my stomach twisting up into knots of anxiety.

Ironside smiles. "They won't be expecting us there," he says. "But don't worry, I don't plan on getting caught. We aren't going to do anything crazy."

"What *are* we going to do?" I question warily.

"We are going to go to your family home, and we will break in," he explains casually.

"What?" I splutter. "Why?"

His eyes are flashing when he gives me the easy, short answer.

"Evidence," he replies.

IRONSIDE

When I need to be up at a certain time, my body doesn't even need an alarm anymore to flip the on and off switches. About five minutes before my alarm is supposed to go off, my eyes open in the pitch blackness of the bedroom, and I'm wide awake.

It's a road trip day, and I can't deny it: the feeling of getting up before dawn to roll out of town on a long ride is one of the best there is. It's eight hours from here to Justine's home town near the Utah-Wyoming border, and there isn't much between here and there besides open road and plains...and Casper, where we'll have to keep a low profile. It's not always easy to know who your friend are, when your enemies are making moves.

I feel Justine still warm against me as I slide out of bed, and I sneak to the bathroom to splash water in my face. I feel my muscles warming up as I stretch and head to the bar to make a pot of coffee, scratching my stubble as I do. I won't bother shaving this morning, partly because I want to save time, and partly because I like the way the wind feels on my face while it's still rough at the start of a trip.

When the coffee pot starts gurgling, I head back into the bedroom and approach Justine's slumbering form, bending over her and scooping her into my arms. She murmurs as I lean forward and kiss her on the neck, then gently working my way up to her cheek and her forehead. When I turn the lamp light on, I see that she's smiling, and I give a low chuckle and kiss her awake on the lips.

"Morning, sunshine," I growl into her ear before she stretches and blinks up at me.

"Urghn," she replies, somehow still cute. "What time issit?"

"We've got a head start on the sun, let me put it that way," I say with a grin.

"Five more minutes," she pleads, turning over in bed.

My hands reach forward and grope her round, soft ass and feel its give as she tries to squirm away from me in her little linen cocoon. Even sleepy and groggy, she gets me riled up faster than anyone I've ever met.

I crawl back into bed with her, and my rough, muscular arms swallow her and pull her into my chest as I grope her breasts and grind against her ass. "I said, it's time to get up. Are you going to give me trouble, little girl?"

"Mhmm," she murmurs candidly, looking smug as she tightens her grip on the sheets and tries to ball up.

"Maybe I ought to wake you up the right way," I growl, "settle down that energy of yours before you're squirming on the back of my seat."

"I thought I smelled coffee," she says in feigned innocence as I slide a hand under the sheets, searching greedily until I find her thigh.

My fingers glide over it and electrify the sensitive skin before they move all the way down between her legs and find her pussy. She tries to hold her thighs together, but I work my way in with hardly any effort and find her clit. While groping one breast through the sheets, I start to rub her clit with two fingers in small, tight circles and feel her gasp and goosebumps pricking up along the back of her neck.

Her mouth hangs open, and she pants softly as my relentless rubbing gets her sleepy body warmer and warmer. I waste no time, sparing her nothing as I torment her clit and feel her honey over my fingers--not a bad way to start the morning, if you ask me.

Now squeezing Justine against me, I feel her shake as the orgasm blossoms from her pussy and spreads through her body. I keep circling her clit while she comes, kissing her on the cheek and nipping her ear between deep, husky breathing.

She rolls over, letting out an overwhelmed breath and looking up at me with wide eyes. "Good morning," she sighs with a warm, blissful smile.

"Alright, brat," I say, chuckling. "Let's get you dressed and head out. We'll want breakfast along the way. It's a long ride to your place."

We pull on our clothes for the day, and Justine watches me slide my kutte over my shoulders. "How do you...*get* one of those?" she asks.

"You're given one when you become a member of the MC," I explain, going to one of my footlockers and opening it to dig around until I find my old green military jacket folded up where I left it. I shake it out and hold it up to Justine, who looks at it with raised eyebrows.

"Here," I say. "This'll keep you safe from the dust on the road."

I slide it over her shoulders, and she blushes as the masculine scent of the crisp jacket surrounds her. She seems comforted by it somehow.

"Thanks," she says, moving her arms around in the comically oversized thing. "It might double as a sleeping bag for me, if I curl up tight."

I snort a laugh and pinch her on the ass. "C'mon, girl, let's hit the road."

An hour later, we're pulling away from the greasy fast food joint on the side of the road a ways outside town, where we stuffed ourselves with a hearty, filling breakfast of sausage patty, egg, and cheese biscuit sandwiches--and at Justine's insistence, a cup of fruit for each of us.

"Sorry it ain't exactly a wholesome, balanced meal," I say with a chuckle as we're about to turn back onto the highway. "We can stop in Casper to pick up something...more up your alley."

"Are you kidding?" she says, and I can hear the grin in her voice. "That was *perfect*. I was starving."

"Damn, ha! I bet all that running around we've been doing took it out of you," I say, grinning back at her.

"Y-yeah, it was the running around that wore me out," she says with a blush, averting her eyes.

I reach behind me and scratch her on the thigh before I roar out of the parking lot, feeling my heart pound and my spirit soaring as I tear across the state.

The first leg of the trip takes us southward to Casper, and with very little between the two, I'm free to let my mind wander. It doesn't wander far-- in fact, it only wanders a few inches to the girl holding onto me in a warm hug.

I feel the same rush I felt back when I first started riding around rural Colorado. Those were the good days, before the military. Those days always felt sunny, and more than anything else, they felt *free*. I couldn't explain freedom--I could describe it, but it was something else to feel it and not know how to share that.

But with Justine here this morning, I can't explain it, but I feel like she shares it with me. The rush of getting up and packing in a quick breakfast for a groggy start comes with a sense of liberty, knowing the road can take you wherever you want, and the entire day is still ripe and fresh before you. That's the feeling that told me I had to be a biker, and even though our destination is grim, we can enjoy the freedom while it lasts.

That's special.

She's special.

By the time we hit Casper, the sun is up and the day is getting busy. My route around the city takes us through some light traffic on the outskirts of the rush hour stream, but I do that on purpose. If we were to drive through the city at a quieter time, we'd be more likely to get spotted. I want to stay as inconspicuous as possible.

We stop to top up on gas on the opposite side of Casper, and just to be on the safe side, I park my bike behind the detached bathroom building after gassing up to let us both answer nature's call.

"Want to stop inside and grab a snack?" I ask before we head in. "Can of coffee for the road?"

"Coffee sounds perfect!" she chimes. "Caffeine makes me talkative though. Be ready for that."

I wink at her and enter the bathroom, chuckling.

As I'm cleaning my hands off inside the stall with a sanitary wipe afterward, though, a sound reaches my ears that makes my heart drop: bike engines. It sounds like they're coming into the gas station, probably to refuel.

"Hey," I say, knocking on the wall between me and Justine. "Hear that?"

"What do we do?" she hisses back through the thin wall. "Wait in here?"

"No, they'll have to come here too," I assure her, frowning. "On three, get out and head straight for the bike, I'll see if I can get us out of here before they notice us."

I count down, and we head out of the stall together and wrap around the building to my bike immediately. Sure enough, I catch a glimpse of the bikers pulling up to get gas, and I recognize some of the faces.

These men belong to my enemy.

I keep still on my bike as I watch carefully from around the corner. After most of the men finish fueling up, they head inside the store, and that's when I take my chance. I pull out as quietly as I can and slip back around onto the highway, then gun the engine and take off in a beeline westward.

Justine holds me tight and leans into me, trusting me fully as she buries her face in my back and sighs contentedly. The adrenaline rush in my veins wakes me up better than a can of coffee ever would have.

Our route doesn't take us *through* the town where I found Justine, but we skirt around the borders of the county along the way. The next time we stop for "lunch" (whatever we can scrounge from a convenience store) a few hours later, I get on the phone with one of our MC's allies in this part of the state, another club that we're on good terms with. After a quick chat with one of their officers, I have intel on which roads are going to be more and less heavily patrolled this afternoon.

And that makes staying covert a hell of a lot easier.

The rest of our trip is more of the same, steering clear of the other outlaws whose colors say we're not on good terms with--most of them connected to Diesel--and avoiding the state troopers that by now must have eyes out for Justine.

Justine has shed the jacket by the time the sun is high in the sky, and it's about noon when we cross the Utah border. And as we do, some of the excitement of the day starts to melt away from her--I can feel it in her touch.

A little over an hour later, the next time I pull over on the side of the road is when we're at the sign showing the name of the town, and beyond it lies a community of probably a few hundred at most. It's a wonder there's anything that big out here at all.

"How do you feel?" I ask her, looking over my shoulder.

"Not great," she admits.

"Here's the plan," I say. "What are your parents' schedules like at this time of day?"

"The house should be empty for another few hours," she says after thinking for a moment.

"Unless?" I ask.

She shrugs, bewildered. "Unless they have a reason to come home, I don't know?"

"If there's evidence that your dad was trying to make you someone's bride against your will," I say, "it'll be at home, where he thinks it's safest. And right now, you're a legitimate runaway as far as he's concerned, so his attention is going to be on finding you. If we're lucky, he hasn't had time to cover his tracks. Are you sure you're ready for this?"

She looks reluctant, but then takes a deep breath and nods. "Yes. I'm not the only girl in this county. Even if we can't put Daddy in jail, I...I want enough to make it public. This happened behind closed doors, and I don't want it to stay that way."

I nod. "You've got a good head on your shoulders, Justine. If your dad were worth shit, he'd be proud of you like I am."

She squeezes me softly. "It's enough that you're proud of me," she says, half-teasingly.

I chuckle, and we pull off again.

Justine's family house is a nice one, I have to admit. It's a cozy two-story home with a tidy yard and a cozy feel to it, despite the otherwise dry environment of the town. Sure enough, there are no cars in the driveway. Still, I park down the block and leave my bike behind a fence sheltered by branches. We need to be quick and not draw attention to ourselves or the house.

Justine leads the way. "I've run through my neighbor's yards all my life," she whispers. "I know how to get us there without getting seen." We weave through dry old trees and crumbling sheds until we reach her own home, where she looks around furtively before going to the back porch and taking out a small work glove from under the stairs.

She dumps the spare key out of it and grins at me as she holds it up. I chuckle and watch her unlock the back door and sneak inside, with me close behind her.

The house is deathly empty. Justine immediately changes once we're inside. Her lip quivers for a moment, but she takes a deep breath and swallows, looking around at the place and taking it all in. I can only imagine what's stewing in her mind.

The decor is kind of quaint and homey, but there's something a little drab about it all I can't put my finger on. It could be the peeling edges of the dated wallpaper, or maybe the faint musty smell of the carpet, but I can see why this kind of place gives her a sense of melancholy.

"Daddy's office is upstairs," she says. "But he keeps it locked."

"Bingo," I say, moving past her and taking out a bobby pin from my pocket.

We head upstairs, past Justine's childhood photos and tense-looking family pictures, and it's hard not to ask her about her past. I want to know everything about her and help her heal, but right now, she's holding it together delicately. I shouldn't interrupt that.

Once we reach the door she points out to me, I carefully pick the lock and get it open in a matter of seconds.

"Holy crap," she says, blinking at my handiwork as I step inside.

"Language, young lady," I say with a wink that makes her blush as I hold the door open for her.

We step inside to what looks like a typical home office, with a desk and a computer on it and shelves of books and award plaques on the walls. I don't know what Justine's father does for a living, and I don't need to. His office tells me enough about his type.

Justine and I begin searching the room. She goes through folders in the drawers while I get on the computer and see what he was looking at last.

I start looking through his emails, sifting through the personal ones until I find one that has language I'm looking for: it's vague, but it seems to be discussing a deal with another person. There's a reference to a contract, and another exchange about it being signed.

"I think I've found your dad's deal," I grunt, stroking my chin, "but he words his emails carefully. I don't know if this is incriminating enough. Let me see if I can find this contract he mentions. There might be a hard copy around here, too."

"I found this that looks recent," she says, taking out a clip of papers and showing them to me. "But it's not signed. It must be a copy."

"Bet he's got it in his car," I grumble. "But he's got to have a backup…"

I start to look through his folders until I find one that's password-protected.

"Is your dad on the older or younger side?" I ask.

"Older," she asks hesitantly. "Why?"

I type in Justine's full name as the password, then just her first name, and a few other combinations until Justine gives me her birth date, and I add that to her first name. The folder unlocks, and I smile as I open it to find…pictures.

Most of them are of documents. In fact, the very first is a copy of the contract Justine is holding, signed by what looks like Justine's father and another man. But while I try to save the emails and the contract picture to a thumb drive, I notice the other pictures that Justine is staring at.

They're of her.

Some of them are modest photos, but others

appear to have been taken without her noticing. Her face pales as she realizes that she might be looking at her own advertisement pictures.

"This one is from when I was in high school," she says with a horrified face, hovering over one."

Before I can respond, both of us freeze at the sound of the door downstairs.

Justine looks out the window, and she puts a hand to her mouth. "It's my mom! S-she must be home for lunch," she whispers to me urgently.

"Come on," I say, taking the thumb drive, closing out of the folders, and crossing the room to the window. "Then we get out of here a different way than we came."

I pull the window open carefully and quietly, and Justine carefully slips out onto the roof. She wobbles on the sloped surface, but I follow her out and keep her steady as we walk cautiously to the corner of the house, where we're able to climb down a metal trellis covered in withered vines.

Our feet hit the ground, and we dart through the backyard, back to the bike, my heart racing as I hold Justine's hand. I don't even stop to look and see if we've been spotted. We race to the bike, hop on, and ride out of the neighborhood like we've just robbed the place.

"Oh my god," I hear Justine breathe behind me. "Oh my god, we just did that."

"Hell yeah we did," I laugh. "Now hang tight,

we're taking a different way back than the way we came, and I'm not stopping until I hit a motel!"

Sure enough, our ride takes us to a motel that's a few notches above the worst I've seen on this side of the border. I paid for a room with one bed, and I took Justine by the hand as I walked her to the room down the open-air sidewalk.

"Hey," I ask, squeezing her hand. "Before I order us pizza, how are you feeling about what we just did?"

"I...think it's going to take some time to set in," she says, giving me an uneasy but loving smile. "But I'm glad we did it before I had time to think myself out of it. Do you...do you think this will be enough to put him away?"

"I think we got our hands on more than he ever expected us to get," I say with a chuckle, patting the thumb drive in my pocket and unlocking the door to the motel room. "You did good today, Justine. Real good. Now get in that bathroom and strip."

JUSTINE

$\mathcal{I}$ wake up from a beautiful dream feeling totally refreshed and relaxed. There's a smile hovering still on my lips as the soft comfort of my dream hangs around me. It was lovely. I was in a swimming pool somewhere tropical, just floating around in the cerulean water. There was a beach within eyesight of the pool, and the sun was warming my face, caressing my bare skin and making me feel alive. Of course, any fantasy would be empty without my handsome captor-turned-savior lounging in the pool with me. In my mind, the image of blue water reflecting dappled light across his gorgeous, rugged face and hard, chiseled body still blooms like a flower. I feel so warm and happy inside, and I can't help but wonder if my dream will ever come true. The idea of traveling the world and seeing beautiful places alongside the man of my dreams is almost too perfect to even imagine. Especially when I compare that dream to the life I have always lived back home. The repression, the boredom, the same routine day in and day out that left me feeling bedraggled and restless at the same time. I never knew how deep my thirst for adventure could reach, but there's just something about being on the road with Ironside that makes me long for different horizons. I want to experience everything this world has to offer, good and bad, and I know I am brave enough to face it all with Ironside next to me, lifting me up, being my constant backup. He makes me feel safe and proud and brave all at once. It's really quite amazing, I think.

I open my eyes and smile at the soft morning light filtering in through the gauzy motel curtains, casting swaying shadows across the bed. I'm tangled up in the sheets next to Ironside, just drinking up the coziness of the moment. It feels oddly domestic, like we've got a routine together even though we're on the road traveling and nothing is *really* routine. Maybe there isn't a kitchen, and maybe we're not putting down roots, but somehow it's like every place I go to with him feels like home. I have a feeling he's taking in a little more luxury and comfort than he would normally choose for himself while traveling-- he's definitely the kind of rugged guy who could sleep rough under the stars and think nothing of it. But having me along for the ride changes things. We stay in motels. We sleep in beds. And every night, I fall asleep under the watchful gaze of my hero. He keeps watch and makes sure nothing and nobody can harm me while I'm vulnerable. And then in the morning, I wake up to find myself curled up in his arms. There is no safer place for me in the world than wherever he happens to be. That much I know for certain. No one can protect me like he can.

I stretch out a little, yawning, and I feel Ironside wake up. He presses a soft kiss against the back of my head, nosing into my hair. It's a lovely, ticklish feeling that makes me tingle from my head down to my toes. I tilt my head back to peer up at him adoringly and he kisses my forehead, too, making me giggle.

"Good morning, sweetheart," he murmurs gruffly against my hair.

"Morning," I reply, my heart exploding with affection for him.

I wriggle back against him, reveling in the wall of hard muscle behind me. No matter how many times I see him naked or touch his glorious body, it never ceases to amaze me. I can't believe he's real. And I definitely can't believe he considers me good enough to be his girl. Because, I realize now, that is what this is turning into. Maybe at first I was simply his charge, his unexpected responsibility. And sure, that is still partly true. He looks after me like a guardian, protects me like a bodyguard-- but he fucks me like a lover. Like we are simply man and woman, free of the clutter of our circumstances. It was an accident that we fell in together, but I am eternally grateful that my rocky road led me to such a beautiful place in the world. All the suffering, all the fear and self-loathing I have endured for so many years, it's all worth the struggle whenever I look at Ironside. Whenever he touches me, it's like he erases the pain underneath my skin. His attention and his protection are bringing me out of my shell into the light, and god, does it feel so damn good.

His arms fall around me possessively and he pulls me in tight to his chest, gently rutting against me so that I can feel that he's already partially stiff. That gives me the same little thrill I get every time. It stuns me to think that my body in proximity to his is enough to turn him on, but I'm learning with awe that he seems perpetually ready to go. He is just as aroused by my presence as I am intoxicated by his. How lucky. How fortunate that we fit together this way.

"How did you sleep, my angel?" he asks. His warm breath washes over my ear and neck, giving me goosebumps. I'm so in tune with every little move he makes.

"Good," I answer. "I had a really nice dream."

"Oh, really? What did you dream about?" he asks idly.

"Oh, it was lovely, Ironside. You and me, lounging around in this pool by the beach. I can still smell the sunscreen and the chlorine. We were close enough to hear the crash of waves on the shore. It was incredible. Do places like that really exist?" I wonder aloud.

Ironside chuckles and squeezes me tight. "Yes, my love. Those places do exist. And if we're lucky, maybe one day we can make that dream of yours come true. I for one would love to see this body in a bikini. I bet you'd melt the pavement. Hotter than the sun," he whispers.

I blush and giggle, trying to squirm away from him.

"Oh, stop. You're making me blush," I laugh.

"Good!" he growls.

He pulls me back and kisses me on the lips before letting me roll out of bed. I stand up and stretch, loving the sensation of the morning sun beaming warmly on my body through the curtains. Ironside props himself up on one elbow for a moment, just watching me.

"God, you're gorgeous," he murmurs, shaking his head.

Suddenly self-conscious, I grab a sheet from the bed and wrap it around my naked body, which makes him laugh softly.

"Maybe one of these days you're going to realize

how beautiful you are," he remarks. "Until then, I'll just have to keep reminding you."

"You're too sweet to me," I reply, beaming.

"I'm exactly as sweet as you deserve," he replies as he slides out of bed. "Come on, darlin'. We need to get back on the road. Let's get cleaned up and roll out."

I dutifully head into the bathroom with him, where we take a shower together and towel-dry off, then get dressed. We pack up and check out of the motel, stepping out into the bright sunshine. Even though I know I should be a little wary every time we're out on the road-- there's no telling what kind of trouble we might run into-- I just feel so exhilarated. Riding on the back of his motorcycle is the closest to a thrill ride I have ever felt. I slink my arms around his waist and let the wind whip through my hair, drying it gradually as we roll along the highway.

We're headed eastward, which I glean from the various road signs we pass. At first, this doesn't really bother me. I trust Ironside to know where he's going and how to protect us both while on the road. But as we start nearing the Utah border, that little forgotten pit in my stomach starts to grow and become more obvious. Fear builds up higher and higher inside of me and I find myself watching the signs pass by with a sense of intense dread. I'm diving right back into the belly of the beast, or so it feels to me. I know I should just trust Ironside, as he's never steered me wrong in the past. But I can't help but react with fear to the idea of being back on my old home turf. There are lots of dark memories here that I have worked very hard to run away from and forget about. Lots of old demons just hanging around the dusty, mountainous state, waiting for me to return. I can feel fear sinking its poisonous claws into me as we ride along, and before long I can't hold back anymore.

"Where are we going? This isn't the way we came," I lean forward and ask, my lips mere millimeters away from the shell of his ear.

He gives my hands a reassuring squeeze and turns his head slightly so I can hear him when he responds. "I know. We're taking the scenic route. I want to show you as much of the world as I can while I've got you, little girl. You stick with me, you will see a lot more. There's so much you haven't seen yet," he says.

It's a fair answer. He's right. I've been so sheltered all my life that I haven't done a lot of exploring, not even in my home state. But I can't fully relax and enjoy the excursion, not with the dread of being in enemy territory still hanging heavily over my head. Still, I do my best to outrun the alarm bells ringing in my head, and I force myself to think of more lovely possibilities. For example, the potential of traveling the world with Ironside. The thought of waking up in a new place every morning, spending our days on the road and our evenings in bed together-- well, I have to admit that it sounds like my idea of heaven. I could spend all my time with this amazing, awe-inspiring man who smells of leather and fuel and adventure. I could gaze into those dark, contemplative eyes every night as I fall asleep. I could learn more about him, teach myself how to better serve and support him as he serves and supports me. We are growing closer and closer together, and I am oddly reminded of a tree that used to grow in my backyard at home. It was an apple tree, but whoever lived on the property before my family must have been a little experimental with the garden, since there was an orange branch grafted onto the apple tree. Miraculously, in a feat I still don't fully comprehend, that tree kept growing. It produces apples and oranges now, which I didn't even know was possible. But it reminds me so much of what I have with Ironside. We are two totally different people. We could hardly have dreamt up such wildly contrasting backgrounds. On paper, we have little in common. But what we do share is an intimate connection unlike any other. We may be different, but together we are stronger. We grow together despite our differences, just like those apples and oranges. We share everything. We support one another back and forth endlessly in a totally symbiotic relationship. Sometimes it feels like

I don't have much to offer him, especially compared to the protection and security he provides for me. But I support him in other ways. I give him affection. I do as I'm told. And at night, I give him a warm, loving body to sleep next to. Maybe it's not much, but it's what I have to offer, and to his credit, he seems perfectly happy to accept that.

As we ride along, I try to think of happier things to keep my mind off of my worries. I close my eyes and rest my cheek against Ironside's muscular shoulder, taking comfort in how strong and powerful he is, how safe I am in his possession. I start to furnish a fantasy world with a life we could one day have together, if all the dark things that pull at us from every direction could just lie still for once. There are so many anchors weighing us down, but if we could just free ourselves from those burdens, we could build such a lovely life together. I even smile to myself thinking about what our potential children might look like. Is that silly? Maybe. But it makes me feel warm and fuzzy inside, so it must be worth it in that regard, at least. I wonder if our children would have his dark eyes or my light eyes. Would they be courageous and fearless like their father or quiet and timid like me? Would they have a powerful love of travel and being on the road like we do? I have to imagine they would, growing up with the kind of life we two could create.

I'm so wrapped up in my lush fantasy world of

the future that it takes me a little while to realize where we're heading. But finally I open my eyes and start reading the signs we pass by, and when my brain clocks those grim words, my heart nearly drops down into my belly. We pass by a sign for the Sunny Hilltop Preparatory for Girls and I feel my blood run cold.

It's a place I rarely revisit in my mind. In fact, my years spent at an all-girls boarding school are some of the fuzziest and most suppressed of all. Terrible things happened there. Nothing overly traumatic, but just awful enough to have forced my brain to put up a soft block against it. The memories are there, but they are blanketed with a thick layer of denial and out-of-sight-ness that help me get through the days since then. It's strange to think about who I was back then. How did I cope with the harsh rule of puritanical teachers, hellbent on policing every little thing I said or did at all times? We were treated like zoo animals there, or like showroom pets. We were paraded around like prized poodles, all of us forced to make ourselves soft and pliant and beautiful. Perfect future brides for uptight men who hate women. Some of my classmates ran away from the place, preferring the unpredictability of life on the streets than the clanging, painful routines of the boarding school. I still feel oddly guilty and disappointed in myself for not being one of those runaways. I was always too afraid, too well-behaved.

But while I didn't physically run away, I can't pretend like I haven't spent years trying to evade Sunny Hilltop in my memories. In fact, the remembrance of those days upsets me so much that I feel tears burning in my eyes. I start to sob uncontrollably, the tears streaming down my cheeks while my body trembles. It doesn't take very long at all for Ironside to notice that I'm panicking. He pulls the motorcycle over on the side of the road and turns around to hug me.

"I know. It's hard," he murmurs. "But you're okay. I got you."

"It's just that… ugh, so many bad memories. I didn't know it would still hurt so badly," I confess to him tearfully.

"Sweetheart, you are so strong," he assures me. "But if we need to, we can drive back the opposite way. I am not going to push you through trauma you don't need."

I sniffle and wipe at my eyes. "No. I need to do this. I need to face up to it."

"I've suffered, too, and I know how difficult it is to face your demons. One word, little girl, and I will turn this bike around," Ironside reminds me.

I manage to give him a smile, even through my tears. "I'm ready. I have you. I can do this. We should at least drive past the place," I mumble.

"Whatever you say, Justine," he says, kissing me softly.

We pull back onto the road and keep going in the direction of the school, my heart beating like crazy. But when we pull up to the place, I am stunned to find that it's all closed down and boarded up. In fact, it looks like it's been that way for a long time. The buildings that once held so much power and fear in me look abandoned, dilapidated. The fences sag. The walls are crumbling. The landscaping, once kept pristine by a combination of groundskeepers and student labor, has become totally overgrown. It's all wild and unruly, a total turnaround from the hallowed halls of rules and regulations it used to be.

"It's dead," I murmur in awe. "It's really dead."

"How are you feeling about it?" he asks helpfully.

I give him a confident smile. "Amazing," I answer.

"Good. Let's explore," he says, giving me a wink.

We park the bike and set out on a little exploration of the old school grounds. Everything is so eerie and quiet. Not even the birds or insects are chirping here. It's all death, all silence. I'm so relieved. It's cathartic getting to walk around the place without the fear of some professor or administrator appearing from the shadows to punish me for some perceived slight or lapse in courtesy. As we look around, I point out various places that used to positively vibrate with dark memories for me. A table in the cafeteria where a mean older girl flipped my lunch tray, sending my food flying messily across the linoleum floor. A corner of the auditorium where a teacher once whacked my knuckles with a ruler for forgetting to put my name on my math homework. And finally, the dorm room where I used to cry myself to sleep in bed.

I look around the deserted room, amazed to find how different it feels now. And as I'm watching the room, Ironside is watching me.

"How do you feel?" he asks again, always attentive to my needs.

"It's weird," I admit. "This place used to scare me so much. It was torture for me."

"Well, you have nothing to fear now," Ironside says. "You're safe. Those days are over."

He saunters over and puts his arms around me, kissing me. When he breaks away, there is a mischievous glint in his eyes. I look at him dubiously.

"What? What is it?" I ask.

He smiles. "We're going to make some much better memories here."

"How so?" I question, tilting my head to one side.

"Which one of these was your bed?" he asks.

I point to it, wrinkling my nose. "That one."

He promptly scoops me up and carries me over to the bed.

"Good. Because I'm going to fuck you in it," he growls.

"I don't like the sound of it already," I growl as we stride through the bar downstairs toward the meeting room, Justine following close beside me while Breaker walks on the other.

"Just because it involves Justine, you assume it's a bad thing," Breaker says with a chuckle. "Well, I think that's up for her to decide."

Before I can open my mouth and protest with a glance at Justine, Breaker pushes the door open and leads us inside. Justine tugs at my hand and stops me at the door, giving me an uncertain look and glancing in at the meeting.

"You're more than welcome at this meeting," I say with a firm nod at her. "At my side. If anyone's got a problem with that, they can take it up with me."

I don't bother glancing around menacingly at the room after that statement. I know nobody here would object. If they would, then they wouldn't be my closest comrades. Tank didn't count, but if he let out so much as a wrong breath her way, I'd drag him behind my bike next time we ride.

Bones, Big Daddy, and Tank are all already in the room, with Tank standing at the end of the table with his hands folded in front of him. He gives us the slightest hair of a nod as we enter, and Breaker takes a seat by Tank while I sit with Justine at the far end.

"I hear you two had a little field trip," Tank says with a coy grin.

"Fuck off," I grunt.

"Must've been a nice ride," Tank murmurs to Breaker, who furrows his brow at him.

"Don't push it, or I'll trade seats with him," Breaker warns, and Tank holds up a hand and chuckles.

"Colorado or Utah?" he asks me. "Damn, the ride down to Grand Junction must be pretty this time of year. You know, if you ever do head that way, you two should check out-"

"Tank," Breaker interrupts.

"Alright, preacher," he says, waving him off. "No jokes in church, I hear ya."

"Cut to the chase, I hear you've got news," I say, leaning forward with a stony frown as Justine subtly scoots her chair closer to mine.

"Wait, I kind of want to hear what he was going to say," she whispers to me, and I roll my eyes.

"We can talk to him later," I assure her, a little curious myself, even though I'd never let it show.

"So, here's the deal," Tank says as Big Daddy takes a long drink of coffee. "Diesel wants you, little lady," he says with a nod to Justine, "real bad." Looking around at the group, he goes on, "Diesel ain't all that happy about that little stunt Ironside pulled at his club. It's an embarrassment. He wants to cover his ass, meaning his reputation."

"Damn right he should," I say, tapping a knuckle on the table. "I've had a harder time breaking into houses than I did at his club. It was like getting in and out of a goddamn grocery store."

"Hey, I'm not here to defend his uh, business model," Tank says. "I'm just saying his ego's bruised."

"Man like Diesel trying to cover his ass is a dangerous thing," Big Daddy says.

"And it makes him act funny," Tank says, nodding. "I passed word on to Diesel that I had eyes on Justine in this county. That got him interested, real fast, and I usually have to do more convincing that something is worth his time. That means he's hungry for a lead."

"A lead *we're* going to feed him?" I ask, cracking a grim smile.

Tank grins and winks. "Bingo, G.I. Joe."

"Can we kill him after we're done here?" Big

Daddy asks Breaker nonchalantly, and Bones snickers.

"Sounds like you have something in mind for this?" I ask, leaning back and crossing my arms, glancing at Justine and trying to think ahead to where she factors into this.

It's impossible not to feel on-guard for her sake. She's got more spirit than I gave her credit for, and although she's still naive, she's got the guts deep down to get her hands dirty, and that's more than I can say for most people. But I don't want her getting tossed around by this crowd.

It might break her her before she even grows into her full potential. I can't let that happen.

"I do," Tank says with a deep breath. "If you want to get Diesel out of hiding and into the open, the best way to do that at this second is that girl right there," he says, pointing a finger at Justine. "Diesel knows I'm in this area. I'll report to him that I snatched Strawberry Blondie over there, and that I'm hightailing it away from *your* club."

"So, that you pulled the same shit I pulled on him?" I ask.

"Exactly," Tank says with a firm nod. "I tell him I don't want to lead him back to his place, and I'll suggest a meeting point we've used before."

"Will he buy that?" I ask, interested so far.

"He'll be suspicious," Tank says, "and that's the catch. I'll need to prove that I've really got her with me when we go to the meeting place. Meaning, send pictures, videos, that kind of thing. He trusts me, but he'll take precautions."

"He's not stupid," Big Daddy admits.

"No," Tank admits, chuckling. "Don't make that mistake. You wouldn't be the first."

"Hell no," I say firmly, putting a hand on Justine's knee.

"See?" Tank says with a frown to Breaker, jabbing a thumb at me.

"Ironside-" Breaker says, but I'm not having it.

"I'm not letting you use her as bait," I growl. "You have any idea what she's been through?"

"Hell of a lot, if she's riding with you," Tank says with a chuckle, and I see red, rising to my feet and getting ready to climb up onto the table and drop kick that smug bastard into the wall.

But I feel a hand on mine.

It's small and soft, and its owner gives me a look that seems to make the anger melt away like snow in the sunshine. It's almost like a drug, it gives me so much pause so quickly. She smiles up at me appreciatively, but I understand her intentions, and I slowly sit back down. She wants to speak for herself, and she has the right to do so. She's not a child.

"Actually," she says, looking around the room at everyone, "I...I want to do anything I can to make sure what happened to me doesn't happen to anyone else. And if that means taking a little risk," she says, looking back up at me, "then I want to at least hear it out."

"I'm not putting you in harm's way," I say firmly, feeling my protective instincts aching between the urge to let her stand on her own two feet and keep her sheltered.

"If we don't have her actually there to deliver," Tank says, "he won't buy it."

"Then we need to think of another way," I insist, slamming my fist on the table. "Think about it. If you fake a hostage exchange with Diesel, *you're* the one who is going to be suspicious, so he'll have guns trained on you--while you're holding Justine. And if they so much as smell anything going wrong, they'll open fire on the both of you."

"Well-" Tank starts.

"And assuming you're a good actor under pressure," I go on, "which you probably are, I'll admit, because you're still alive so far-"

"Thanks," Tank slips in quickly.

"Then you still have Justine right in the middle of where we'd need to be opening fire from cover wherever we're hiding. She's in too many crosshairs at too many times for too many things to go wrong."

"You got a better idea, Drill Sergeant?" Tank snarls. "I'm all ears."

"Matter of fact, I do," I say firmly, standing up and putting my hands on the table to cast a glare around at everyone. "And Prez, you'll have to excuse me for talking club business around outsiders, but when we crossed back into Wyoming from Utah, we left three bodies of Diesel's men behind us. No one left to report back, but it'll only be a matter of time before they check that patrol route when those three don't check in."

"I assume you've got a good reason for that," Breaker says earnestly. "But that does mean we should expect revenge. And soon."

"Exactly," I say, nodding. "I crossed paths with 'em by chance and had no choice but to do what I did if I wanted to make it out of Utah alive. If Tank weren't here and we were on our own, my first thought would be to get Justine out of the state and far away from here, immediately."

"That's true," Breaker agrees, nodding and crossing his arms. "It's the move I'd make, too."

"And it's probably the one Diesel is going to anticipate," I say carefully, pointing a finger at Tank. "So when *you* go back to Diesel and give him a tip that Breaker is about to personally move Justine across state lines…"

"He'll grab the bait," Tank admits, crossing his arms and frowning but nodding.

"But then we're just setting up a bloodbath," Bones points out. "When they move to intercept, we might not have Justine with us, but they won't come in small numbers, they'll come with the whole damn pack."

"What if we offer to trade me for a ceasefire?" Justine speaks up, and the men stop and look at her.

She blushes under the sudden attention of the room, but she clears her throat and speaks. "Diesel wants me, and he just...lost...a few people, didn't he?"

"He might be willing to bargain for the kind of money that would mean he could make in peace," I admit, frowning. "That's not a bad idea, but..."

"I don't have to be in the line of fire," she says, looking up at me with determination in her eyes, "but I'd be on your side, and it would let you both show up thinking you're there to make peace, not fight, right?"

"Maybe a biker with a short lifespan might think that," Tank says with a snort.

"He'll come armed," I agree, "and on guard, but we'll be able to set the stage before he gets there. That meeting point you mentioned, Tank, he'll assume he's comfortable there. We could use that. Justine," I ask, looking down at her and squeezing her hand. "You'd better be sure that you know what you're suggesting. And you'd better know I'm not going to leave your side for a second," I add, tightening my grip on her hand.

She has a resolute, stubborn look on her face when she looks up at me, and I realize if I don't meet her halfway, we won't get anywhere here.

"Wouldn't have suggested it if I wasn't ready for it," she says.

"We can keep her in cover," Bones suggests, "so they can see her and put 'em at ease, but she can be out of the way."

"The place I have in mind is a mine shaft," Tank says, nodding and stroking his chin. "That...would work perfect, I think."

Justine smiles smugly up at me.

"Alright," I say, relenting and putting a hand on her shoulder. "But I'm keeping you on a short leash."

"Big problem with that," Breaker says, shaking his head. "Hate to burst your bubble, kid, but Diesel knows how much I hate human trafficking. It's kind of our 'thing.' The Heartbreakers were born from a literal fight to stop it. Diesel would see through it."

Glancing down at Justine, I give a subtle nod and an assuring smile before looking at Breaker. "You're right," I say, "he'd see right through it if *you* were offering a ceasefire. But if *I* were the one doing it behind your back, to stop a feud before it turns hot..."

"Diesel wants blood, but he likes money more," Tank says, and Breaker sighs, but he finally nods to me firmly.

"Let's do it," he says. "Make the call."

There is a heavy feeling hanging in the air, dead weight bearing down on my shoulders, making me feel like gravity is focusing on me in particular. I'm sitting on the bed, body tensed and head swimming with confused, panicked thoughts I can't seem to rein back in no matter how hard I try. Across the room, lit by a pillar of golden afternoon haze, Ironside is perched on the edge of a chair. He's dressed in his usual attire, his dark hair slicked back and wet after a shower. It's slowly drying, just like mine. In this pause before the leap we're supposed to take tonight, we have been subconsciously seeking out those little things that help calm us. For Ironside and me, that's been a hearty breakfast and a long, leisurely shower together. We took our time cooking this morning, frying up a stack of eggs and bacon that could rival the output of a brunch restaurant on

a Sunday. The others greatly appreciated our handiwork, but it was still very apparent that nobody was
able to fully enjoy the meal at our proverbial breakfast table. There's nothing but long faces here at the
clubhouse. We can skirt around it. We can pretend
nothing is going wrong. We can put on a brave face
and proceed as normal, but that doesn't change the
fact that tonight we are facing the beast itself. Every-
body knows the risks. And we all prepare ourselves
in different ways, including the gorgeous man across
the room from me.

In his hands is possibly the most frightening
object I have ever seen: a gun. A big one. Black and
shiny, made even shinier by the thorough polishing
and cleaning Ironside has been giving it. His handsome face is slightly contorted, twisted into a grim
expression. His heavy brows are knitted and
furrowed, his sensual lips pressed into a hard line. I
can tell he's focused on the task at hand, but there is
a part of him that's spinning out a complicated web
of thoughts beyond even my perception.

He's thinking about what we are about to do,
what we are all gearing up for. Because the heavy
sensation is not contained to just this room-- the
whole clubhouse is positively thrumming with it.
Everyone is on the same page. We all know exactly
what needs to be done, after the update we received
from our mole on enemy territory yesterday. The
tension is so thick in this building you could pretty

much slice it with a knife. Today is the deep breath before the great plunge, the eye of the storm in which we are all caught and suspended, hanging in mid-air with simultaneously too much and not enough to do and no way to fully prepare for the game plan ahead of us. Off and on throughout the day, my heart has been alternating between panicked racing and a steady, resolved rhythm. It's like my body can't figure out whether to fight or flight or just relax. After all, we have a little time before we go into battle. But that time isn't comfortable. It's the anxious, silent countdown to something potentially dangerous. Well, no-- more like definitely danger-ous. Potentially deadly. Though, of course, I'm trying my hardest not to think about it that way. Strangely enough, it's not even really fear for myself that has me rocked. I will be the bait, a fact that still hasn't fully sunken in for me yet. I'm worried about Iron-side, about his club family, about the ruse we are setting up to trick Diesel. If something goes wrong, there's no telling how severe the situation could become. There are so many variables to consider, and many of them beyond our control entirely.

So here we are, sitting here in this room, both of us trying to think about absolutely anything but the challenge ahead. I lean back against the pillows, stretching out my legs as I watch Ironside put aside one gun and start cleaning and loading the next one. His hands smooth along the sleek metal base, artfully using a rag and cleaning solution to make sure the weapon is in working order. Personally, I have always had a bit of a block up when it comes to guns. Weapons in general just tend to make me nervous. I don't like the idea of causing anybody pain, much less intentionally endangering someone's life. I know the men we will be dealing with are bad guys. I understand that, and I am starting to figure out that some people are just bad-- not worth the time to convert. There was a time when I believed all people were good on the inside, even in the face of evidence to the contrary. But ever since what happened with my father, it's harder for me to make excuses for people, especially bad men. So much of the grief I have endured was at the hands of men.

Though I have to admit to myself that there is one man I know will never let me down, and he is sitting across the room from me. And my god, he looks like a dark angel with the afternoon light spilling generously over his striking form. The way he handles his weapons reminds me of the way he handles my body-- with caution and care, but also with a sexy sense of self-assurance that shines through in every little thing he does. I get the feeling that Ironside is the kind of guy who pretty much always knows what he's doing. He keeps cool-headed and steady-handed in every situation, even when things are tense. The way he lied so smoothly to that cop who was looking for me still amazes me.

And the way he cleans his guns makes my heart race a little faster. I hate to admit how hot he looks right now, but it's true. Part of it is mechanical, watching those hands carry out a menial task with such rugged elegance and swagger. But I know another part of the appeal is the image that he has things under control. He knows how to hold a gun. He knows how to pull the trigger and I know he's not afraid to do it if the situation requires it. In fact, I have a feeling he might even be better-equipped to handle a gun than the other guys are, and that's saying something.

So maybe, I should say something. You know, since this could be our last time spent together. I have no way of knowing what tomorrow holds, but for now, we're both here. Might as well make the most of it, right?

"You look hot as hell cleaning that gun," I tell him, already blushing at the way those dirty words feel in my mouth.

Ironside slowly raises his gaze to meet mine, and when his dark eyes lock on me, I feel dizzy. He's so handsome it almost makes me nervous. I remember something my mother once told me years ago… "There's nothing more dangerous on this earth than a good-looking man."

Maybe she's right, but I'm embracing the danger. Why not? As far as I'm concerned, the world as I know it could end tonight.

"And you look pretty as a peach sitting in that bed," he tosses back, along with a breezy smile that could make a nun swoon.

"You know how to handle one of those, huh?" I ask, gesturing broadly toward the gun.

"I can handle any of them," he answers confidently. "Or all of them."

"Impressive. I can't say I've come across that kind of knowledge in my years on earth," I reply with a soft smile. "You've lived a different life than me."

"Ain't that the truth," he sighs. "You know, I don't talk about this all too often. Really, not at all. But what the hell, the future is never promised, so here goes. You want to know what kind of life taught me how to handle all these guns? Well, there's a big stretch of coast in northern Africa where those memories got made. I was barely old enough to join up, but they let me in. I guess they saw something in me."

"They?" I ask, tilting my head.

He stares at the window, but his gaze looks much more distant.

"The Marines," he answers. "I was young and starry-eyed. Just a dumb kid. Thought I was gonna save the world. Yeah, they loved that. Right off the bat, they had me in the tropics: sweating my ass off, carrying a gun bigger than some people's kindergarteners, fighting every day just to stay alive to see tomorrow."

"Why were you sent there? What happened?" I ask, turning to face him more directly.

"There were these smugglers causing big trouble in the region. Not just your run-of-the-mill black market smugglers bringing contraband items across international borders, either. They were smuggling humans," he explains.

My eyes go wide. "Oh god," I murmur.

Ironside sets down the gun and steeples his fingers, peering at me with a glint in his eye.

"There are very bad people in this world, Justine. I know them. You know them. Bad people are everywhere. Sometimes, you don't know who to trust. I mean, I don't have to tell you about that," he says pointedly.

"My own father let me down," I mumble.

"Exactly," Ironside says. There's a softness, an apology in his tone. He understands. Of course, he does. He goes on. "It's important to make sure you're putting in what you're getting out. Trust is a two-way street, and it's the number one thing that can make or break a family. When I got sent off to North Africa, I had to find a new family. At first, I tried to go it alone. I thought I could tough it out. I was always athletic and outdoorsy, anyway. But I wasn't used to that kind of responsibility. They had me searching out the worst of the worst. Drug and sex traffickers, all with blood on their hands. I learned real quick that the only way I was going to survive was if I banded together with my brothers in arms. So, we did. We formed a pack. We did everything as a pack-- it's true what they say about having safety in numbers."

"How long were you there? How did you get out alive?" I press him.

"I lost count of the days. Time means something different when you're at war. Sometimes it felt like we'd been there a week, sometimes it felt like years. Then, one day, we went off on a mission. We'd been on lots of missions before. We knew what we were doing, or so we thought. But the enemy took us by surprise. Even after all that time, we were still at a disadvantage on that terrain. A close buddy of mine went down out of nowhere while we were stalking through the woods. Just dropped to the ground like a fruit fly. At first, I thought he tripped over a tree root. I turned around with a big grin on my face, ready to tease him for falling. But then I saw his eyes. They were just... lifeless. Empty. This friend of mine, he was a big jokester, always messing around. We all spent so much time together and things could get pretty damn dark, but he always had a look in his eye that made us laugh. All he had to do was look at me sideways and I'd crack up laughing. But then he was on the ground and that... that light in his eyes was just put out. All dark. No stars," he growls, shaking his head.

"Oh my god. What happened to him?" I breathe.

"He was shot. Sniped clean from a distance. They picked him off like he was a bright red target. I remember the sound of it. Sharp and high-pitched, not like you'd think. Maybe it was a trick of the wind or something, but I remember thinking it sure didn't sound like a bullet. But it was. A bullet right through his temple. Killed him instantly. My friend, my brother, he was dead before his body even hit the ground. I guess I can thank god for that, at least. He went quick," he relays. "'Course, there's no good way for the good to die young."

"I'm so sorry," I tell him fervently. "That must have been so hard."

"That mission, as you can probably imagine, went belly-up from there. That same mission, I caught shrapnel in my sides. That's where I got my nickname. Ironside. Yeah, they got me good, but I got out of there. I got to come home mostly in one piece. My buddy didn't get to do that. Sometimes, I still think that bullet was meant for me. I was the one in front. I was the first domino that should've fallen. But it was him. I don't understand why he had to die and I got to live. I guess I'm still figuring that out," he says with a shrug.

I slowly slide off the bed and saunter over to him, draping my arms over his shoulders. I gaze into his deep, dark eyes. I can see the pain there, but also strength. So much strength. He looks back at me unapologetically, unabashedly. There's no hesitation to the way he loves me. I rest my forehead softly against his, feeling his body heat wash over me. His hands slip down my sides, lingering around my hips and sloping back to grope my ass. A little moan of surprise escapes my lips and he tilts his face to kiss me. I melt into him, my body folding around to straddle him on the chair. I feel his fingertips drag up my ticklish spine and the back of my neck, pushing up into my hair to softly grasp a fistful. He lightly tugs to pull my head backwards and slightly to the left, making it easier for him to dive in and kiss my exposed neck and collarbone. I shiver and sigh. Goosebumps appear on my skin. He starts to rut against me, slow and intentional. His lips suck bruising kisses into my skin, and his teeth graze the blooming marks.

We take our time stripping off our clothes. We need this. We need a break. Tonight is a gigantic question mark, but for now, we have all we need.

"Come on, little girl. It's time to roll out," Ironside says.

"I'm coming," I assure him as I pull on a pair of boots and slide off the bed.

I follow him up the stairs to the bar, where the others are waiting for us so we can leave. Outside, night has fallen. The darkness has settled in, and it's time to make our move.

"You all good?" Big Daddy growls, looking around the room.

"We're good," Ironside tells him.

"Let's go," says Bones.

My heart is racing as we walk out of the clubhouse and into the crisp evening air. The moon is hanging high and luminous overhead, which I decide to take as a good sign. Why not? I could use a good luck charm tonight. We carefully mount our respective motorbikes and I take my usual spot behind Ironside. I wrapped my arms around him and held on tight as we rode out onto the dimly-lit back roads. We keep on moving through the night, putting a fair amount of distance between ourselves and the relative safety of the clubhouse.

After several hours, we end up at Sherman Hill, a ghost town from the mining boom a few miles south of the Wyoming border. I can feel the change in the air, the tension riding higher as we dismount our bikes and take our places. The gang rolls in around the flank the outside of the mine shaft entrance, where the prescribed trade-off is supposed to go down. I walk to the opening of the shaft with Ironside, my body tingling with nervousness. My eyes dart around as I clock a conveniently-placed nook in the rock formation that could possibly serve as a hiding place in a pinch. We all settle in and prepare for the inevitable meet-up. Half an hour later, after a brief whispered pep talk, Ironside checks his phone with a grim look on his face. Then, he says something to me that strikes an even deeper thread of fear into my heart.

"I suppose this is as good a time as any to tell you my real name," he hisses. "It's Dax. That's my name. Maybe it won't matter soon anyway, but now you know."

"That is not super comforting," I whisper back.

But he doesn't wait to give me a response. He ducks out of the way as Diesel himself, the man at the center of the tornado ripping through our world, comes stalking down the sloping path toward the mine shaft entrance where I stand, positively quaking in my boots.

He is somehow even more intimidating than I pictured before. He's a huge guy with a dead-eyed glare and a permanent snarl to his lip. He looks like the villain of every fairy tale I read as a little girl, and there's no doubt in my mind that when he looks at me, he sees me dead. His entrance is made even more frightening by the men flanking him on either side. There's Tank, our mole, on one side. He looks pissed and ready to fight, and it's hard for me to remind myself he's supposed to be one of us.

And on the other side of Diesel is a man I never expected to see again. It takes a moment for my panicked mind to place where I know him from, and when I do, the terror that grips me is nearly enough to bring me to my knees. I know him. He's the officer who ran the club where I was held captive. Into my mind, a vision thrusts itself onto center stage.

I'm looking at his face, and he is looking at the dead girl.

He's the one.

IRONSIDE

I feel Justine's hand dart to my wrist and grasp it just as Diesel rounds the corner.

The rest of the men have already gotten into their positions in advance. I sent men ahead of us, both in the mineshaft and in some of the old shacks around the circle of dirt road in front of the entryway up to the mineshaft where I'm standing with Justine.

A couple of our newer members are on foot at our side. It would look too suspiciously stupid of me to show up alone with the girl, and if I'm pretending to be committing treason against the club, it would make sense that I have co-conspirators. But we have more of an advantage than I'm letting on, and that's the only way I feel safe having Justine anywhere near the bastard on that bike.

Diesel is a wide, thick man with a broad face,

small, beady eyes, and a buzz cut that doesn't hide the veins running up his muscular neck. He's taller than either of the men riding at his sides, and his presence *feels* bigger. If Buzz hadn't been killed when he had, Diesel would have been likely to make a move to seize power before much longer.

But that was ancient history, and Diesel was just a boy then, like many of us had been. Years have passed. The Diesel that rides before me has a flag bandana covering his head--colors he doesn't deserve to fucking wear--and his bull nose ring glints in the bright moonlight overhead. As he comes closer, I see some of the tattoos on his forearms, and some of the symbols I recognize make my blood boil.

Resisting the urge to try to take a shot at Diesel right here and now is too damn tempting, but for the simple fact that all of this would be for nothing if I missed that moving target, I resist the urge.

"It's him," Justine whispers at my side, her voice suddenly thin like it had been when I first yanked her from the club.

"What?" I hiss.

"The guy at Diesel's side," she breathes with wide eyes, taking a step back, toward a rocky outcropping I'm glad to see she also noticed on the way up here. "He's from the club. I remember him! I-I think he killed the other girl!"

"His name's Dice," I growl, eyes flitting back to

him. "Don't worry. Keep calm. We'll get through this. I've got you. When I tell you, run for that nook, and I'll cover you."

"Okay," she whispers, and Diesel rides up to the end of the last stretch of road, leaving about fifteen feet between us when he and his two officers--Tank and Dice--come to a halt. The other handful of riders hang further back, most of their eyes panning the area around them.

I pray the club can keep hidden well.

"Ironside," Diesel's chain smoker voice says as he chuckles and brings his bike to a stop, dismounting slowly as he looks to Justine and drinks in the sight of her with his eyes. "Long time no see. Both of you. And to tell you the truth, I figured the next time I'd be looking at either of you is down the barrel of a gun," he adds too casually to be a bluff.

"I was acting on Breaker's orders when I got the girl, Diesel," I say, staying professional and straightforward. "Unless Tank has been misinforming you. Don't think I want in on your damn pimping ring, that's not what I started riding for. And we've both lost too many men here--and for what?" I say, feigning a cruel look down at Justine that hurts me even to fake.

"Military boys, those are the real pragmatic minds," Diesel says with a chuckle, glancing at both of the men at his side. "I did my homework on you, brother. Dishonorable discharge. Sounds like you had a disagreement with someone. I can understand that. Always thought you should have stuck around with Buzz, Ironside. You reminded me of him a lot."

I feel sick to my stomach, and I restrain my grimace.

"So," Diesel says as the three stand in front of their bikes in a row, "let's talk terms."

"She goes with you, and I walk," I say, "and we settle our personal feud. Man to man, take this as a gesture of goodwill."

"Goodwill, huh?" Diesel says, raising an eyebrow.

"Three of your men got in my way and went down before they even knew what was happening," I say, my tone straightforward. "You take her back, and I'll steer Breaker away from this warpath of his. War doesn't make money, not for bikers."

Diesel nods, putting his hands on his hips. "You're right about that," he says. "Sure does make me feel better, though."

In the blink of an eye, he pulls a pistol from its holster and fires it...at Tank.

Tank's eyes go wide as the bullet goes into his side, and Diesel fires a second shot into his thigh, and Tank's mouth falls open as his heavy frame collapses to the ground. He bites his wrist to keep from screaming in pain as Diesel laughs.

"You honestly had me on the ride over here," Diesel says with a sick grin. "But a little birdie tipped me off about ya boy Tank. But I figured I'd see it through and get three birds with one stone. Kill 'em both!" he roars at his men, and as we both draw our weapons and my adrenaline lets my mind do what it knows how to do, I'm in motion.

The second he even touched the pistol, Justine was halfway to her hiding place. It's the most valuable cover on our side, and that's why she and only she needs to be in there. When I saw she went one direction and Diesel was aiming at me, I lunged in the opposite. The gun fires, but the bullet hits the mineshaft entrance behind me as I hit the ground and dart for cover as hell breaks loose.

The bikers behind Diesel spread out to cut off our escape, but as they do, the Heartbreakers roar out from cover like a swarm. Immediately, gunfire on both sides breaks out as the bikers begin to roar around the ghost town, surrounding the mineshaft with thunder on all sides.

Dice takes aim at where I'm taking over behind a boulder and fires off a few rounds that ricochet off the rock. He must be keeping me under cover while Diesel gets to his bike. Goddamnit, I can't let Diesel get away from this, not when the plan is already crashing down around our ears!

I crawl to the other side of the boulder and know that as soon as I appear, I've only got a second or two before that gunfire is back on me. I have to make this count.

My legs move me with a swiftness I've never felt

before, and I bolt out from cover toward a broken-down mine cart. As I run, I swing my aim to the bikes, where sure enough Diesel is in the process of mounting his bike to take off. I don't have time to pick a body part. I fire.

"Fuck!" Diesel roars as my bullet hits him through the chest, and he clutches himself, but he still kicks off as his engine roars to life and carries him away from the fray, blood in the sand where he stood as I try to get another shot after him.

But at this range, it's too likely I'd hit another one of the Heartbreakers to risk taking a shot. That, and Dice is already on me, and he *knows* I just hit his Prez.

Dice's bullets shatter pieces of the rusted-through metal as he fires at me, and I realize I need better cover. Suddenly, I see my chance as Dice look to the south in alarm.

Big Daddy has just ridden down one of Diesel's men, a metal baseball bat in his hand, and he takes a swing at Dice that hits him in the bicep before he can dive out of the way. I hear him cry out in pain as he hits the ground, and Big Daddy cackles as he rides by.

But before I can grin and laugh at his blood-thirstiness, I see a couple of Diesel's prospects running forward, trying to storm toward me armed with a tire iron and hunting knife, respectively.

I'm out of bullets, and I don't have time to reload--fuck!

I stow my gun and wait for the one with the tire iron to come close enough for me to lunge at him. He's vicious, but he doesn't have formal training. I get a leg around the back of his knee and have him crumpling to the ground in an instant. But as I'm wrestling the tire iron from his hand, the man with the knife bolts past me toward...Justine!

My instincts make me move faster than I knew my body could move. Having yanked the tire iron from his hand, I swiftly bring it down on the back of his head and feel him go limp in my arms before I get to my feet as I surge forward as quick as I was at the height of my training.

Justine is watching his approach with wide eyes, but I close the distance between us with several long strides and wrap the tire iron around his neck, catching him mid-stride. It gags him as I yank it back, and before he has even hit the ground, I raise my arm and Justine averts her eyes before I bring it down on the bastard.

"Oh my god!" Justine breathes.

I stoop down and pick up the fucker's knife from his limp hand, and I carefully wrap Justine's hand around it and look at her seriously as the sound of gunfire, motorcycle engines, and shouting curses roars behind me.

"Go into the mineshaft," I instruct her, "hide just

inside the entrance, and keep this close. Keep it pointed *out.* I'm not letting this fight get to you."

She nods fervently, and I take out the pistol strapped to my leg and kiss her fiercely before running out to what feels like a battlefield all over again.

I have to maintain my thoughts and stay focused as the fray below. I take out my pistol as I crouch low behind a rock formation that gives me a good view of the fighting. Big Daddy rides around the outskirts of the fighting, swinging his bat around at anyone who dares try to escape, and I spot Breaker in time to see him pull another man off his bike and put a bullet in his head.

I take aim, and when I see one get far enough from the rest of the pack, I take the shot. One, two, three riders I've crossed paths with before go down by my bullets, one whose bike rides straight ahead into another's.

We're winning the day, but I don't celebrate the loss of life. These men chose a dark path, and that's a stain on the reputation of bikers everywhere. For that, I won't lose sleep for putting them down. But seeing combat in my youth taught me one clear thing: the good in people is worth mourning, even if it's lost.

My ear catches the sound of something behind me. I whirl around in time to see-

"Dice!" I roar, seeing red as he barrels right for the mineshaft entrance.

He had been behind my line of fire before I even got into position! Big Daddy had broken the hell out of that arm, but Dice must have been a tougher motherfucker than I thought. He runs for the shaft, probably running for cover from me, but he's about to run directly into Justine's hiding place.

I raise my gun and fire, but the shot misses and hits the rock above the shaft. Dice ducks down and rushes in, and I hear Justine shriek. My heart plummets, and my face goes white as I sprint for the mineshaft breathlessly.

I freeze when I reach the entrance.

Dice is leaning forward, hunched over, and I hear him groan as Justine turns and pushes him aside, off her bloody knife moments before she drops it with a look of shock on her pale face. Dice ran blindly into the mineshaft and right into Justine's knife. And that is a gut wound. He's not getting up from that.

I rush forward to Justine and hug her, and she clings to my body desperately as I look down to Dice with my gun trained on him.

"Should have killed you instead of her!" he snarls as he raises a pistol, but I've already seen it and taken aim at his head.

A single shot, and Dice is dead.

Justine buried her face in my chest before the shot, but she feels the weight off her shoulders all the same. Immediately, she melts into sobbing as I wrap my arms around her and hold her comfortingly, stroking her hair, shushing her.

"I've got you," I whisper. "You did great, baby. You did so great. You're safe now. It's over."

"Is it?" she asks, sniffling as she hugs me and finally looking up at me, trying to regain some of her composure...without much success.

"Diesel rode off with a bullet in his chest," I say, frowning, "and I don't know what kind of damage it did. Don't know if the bastard even has a heart to hit. But the boys are cleaning up outside."

As I speak, I hear the sound of footsteps approaching the entrance to the mineshaft. Both of us turn to look, and my hand grips my gun tightly...before Big Daddy appears, a grin on his face as he twirls his bat around.

"Any foul balls wander down here by chance?" he asks with a wink, and we grin as we step out to the battlefield with him.

What I walk out to is more serious than most of the biker conflicts I've been through in my time on the roads. Bikes and bodies litter the ghost town, with what looks like nearly all of Diesel's men devastated, and a few losses on our own side.

Bones, Breaker, and the three of us close in around Tank's body as the other members start to clean up the scene. We look down grimly at the fallen man, and I feel my heart sinking as I step forward to stoop down in front of him while Bones does the same from behind, inspecting his wound.

"So goddamn close," Breaker says bitterly. "If just one fucking snitch could have kept his mouth shut..."

I felt the burden of guilt weighing heavily on me. Tank and I had butted heads, and I wasn't a friend of his by any measure, but as always, I can't help but wonder if my influence in our plans are part of what got him killed. Justine puts a hand on my shoulder, and once again, I feel that peace I wish I'd had back in the military.

I wish I'd been able to realize I can't predict what *could* have happened. If you punish yourself for doing that, you'll bury yourself alive in guilt every time you fail. That sure as hell happened to me.

Bones winces at the bullet wound, hand on the back of Tank's neck as he turns him over, and he freezes. Bones furrows his brow and puts two fingers to Tank's wrist, and his eyes widen as he looks up to us.

"Holy fuck," he says. "We need to get him to a hospital--he's got a pulse!"

"Oh my god, right there," I moan as a bead of hot water tracks down my cheek.

"Not yet, baby," my handsome hero growls in my ear. "Not until I say so."

I tilt my head back and let the shower spray roll across my body, and I rest my head back against Ironside's chest. His muscular arms are draped around me, holding me up as he grinds his hard cock against my plush little ass. His left hand gropes my breasts, massaging my stiff pink nipples between his thumb and forefinger, while his right hand is between my legs. His fingers press a soft, tantalizing circle around my swollen clit. Tingles of intense pleasure shoot up through my body like forks of bright lightning, making me shudder and tremble in his tight embrace. He's been teasing me like this for several minutes, just feeling me up and carefully taking me right to the edge, then backing off again to make me beg for more.

"Please," I murmur, my chest rising and falling hard with every shuddering breath.

"How badly do you want it, little girl?" he snarls.

"So bad. I need it. I'm so close," I whimper.

"I want you desperate," he hisses against my ear. "I want you on your knees."

"Anything you want," I reply eagerly.

I push back away from him and whirl around, dropping to my knees in front of him. I put up one hand against the steamed-up glass door to steady myself before I lean in and wrap my other hand around his thick cock, stroking and pumping his full length. I look up at him to see his dark eyes locked on me, desire clearly written across his face. His lips are slightly parted, his dark brow furrowed as he watches me. His hands come down to tangle in my damp hair, coiling his fingers around to tug me closer.

I breathe in his deep, masculine scent. It makes my whole body feel a hundred times hotter. Goose-bumps prickle up on my skin and my toes curl instantly I'm desperate to taste him. I need to feel his thickness stretching my cheeks, making it ache so good. I lean in and flick my tongue over the engorged head of his cock before diving in to suck him hard. The sensation of his thick weight on my tongue, pressing into the back of my throat, is nearly enough to make me come alone. I open up my throat and bob up and down, guided lightly by his hair pulling. I swirl my hand around his slick, drippy cock in tandem with my mouth, moaning and sighing as he slowly fucks my throat. I let my hand slip down to fondle his balls every third stroke, keeping up a steady rhythm just how I know he likes.

"Fuck, your sweet little mouth is so good," he groans, pressing me down hard on his cock. I feel a sharp lick of arousal when I taste his salty precome on my tongue.

"Mmm," I moan, letting my lashes flutter as I take him down to the hilt.

Just the feeling of his cock in my mouth makes me so wet, knowing that I can give him the kind of pleasure he deserves. It's a duty I take very seriously. Maybe there are some parts of my father's training that I can use to my benefit. I'm good at taking orders, especially when they come from Ironside.

"You love it when I fuck your throat, don't you, baby?" he purrs.

"Mhmm," I whimper, my mouth stuffed full.

"That's right. You take it so good," he growls, and a shiver rolls down my spine.

I love it when he tells me I'm doing a good job. I live for that feeling. What can I say? I'm an over-achiever, and it's easy to work hard when it's so much damn fun.

I tremble when he pushes me back gently and his cock slides out of my mouth with a slick pop. He takes his cock in his hand, wrapping his fingers over mine as he lightly taps the swollen head against my soft cheek. I peer up at him coyly, biting my lip. He gives me a handsome smirk that damn near melts me into a puddle, then he snaps his fingers for me to stand up. He pulls me in close and kisses me hard on the lips, letting his hard shaft slide wetly across my thigh. I rub against him, always wanting to be closer. Needing to be closer.

"You want me to fuck your tight little pussy until you come again and again?" he whispers against my lips.

I nod fervently. "Yes. Oh god, please," I beg.

"Turn around for me, angel," he hisses, grabbing me by the hips and spinning me around.

I reach out and brace myself against the shower wall with both hands. I need to hold on tight, because Ironside takes no prisoners when it comes to sex. His hands slide down to grope my ass before spreading my legs apart. He slides his cock along the crease between my ass cheeks, teasing me from behind while I wait for him to fuck me, trembling all over. He circles my clit with the head of his cock, tantalizing me to new heights. I back up against him, wiggling my ass. He gives it a hard, resounding slap that stings like heaven.

I cry out and shudder as he chooses that exact

moment to slide his cock inside me, sheathing himself fully inside me in one movement. With just this one stroke, my overstimulated cunny explodes with orgasm, drenching his cock in my thick honey.

"Oh my god!" I whimper, and Ironside has to grab me with both arms to hold me up as he continues to pound into me harder and faster, not letting up for even a second as I come over and over, again and again, just like he said I would.

"Yes! Yes! Yes!" I scream, thankful that we have our own apartment now.

"That's right, Justine, be as loud as you want," he growls appreciatively.

It's all I can do to hold on and stay upright while his cock spears into me so deep I can feel it aching all through my body. His cock pistons in and out, striking my g-spot with every perfect stroke. I reach back to hold onto him and his arm wraps with mine, holding me suspended while he fucks my pussy mercilessly. I lose count of the orgasms sometime after six, just letting him obliviate my mind and use my body. Finally, with a deep groan and a slap of my ass, he comes inside of me. His body seizes up and he holds me in place, emptying himself completely. I clench my aching cunny, eager to get every last precious drop.

Afterward, he slides out of me and we lovingly wash each other off, basking in the afterglow together. We dry off and put on our respective silky robes, heading into the kitchen to make dinner. This has become our routine ever since we got our own place and I love every second of it. I loved being at the clubhouse, but I have to admit Ironside is right about this being so much better. He wants me to be comfortable, to feel at home for the first time in my life, and even though we haven't been here long, it already feels that way. But it wouldn't make a difference where I am, really. As long as Ironside is with me, I'm home.

We take our time making a delicious dinner of homemade pasta and slow-simmered tomato basil sauce, dancing in the kitchen and sipping big glasses of wine. While we're waiting for the water to boil, Ironside brings in his laptop.

"Come here, Justine," he says, beckoning to me. "I have something you ought to see."

Immediately, I feel a flicker of anxiety. "Oh no. What is it?" I ask warily.

He gives me a reassuring smile. "It's not a bad thing, angel. I promise."

I reluctantly walk over to watch as he pulls up a news recording of a highly publicized arrest... and the man in shackles is familiar.

In fact, he was once family.

My father.

"Oh my god," I gasp, clapping a hand over my mouth.

"It worked, little girl. We did it. We got him," Ironside says, kissing me on the cheek.

"Our evidence?" I breathe.

"It had to have helped," he says.

After we handled the situation with Diesel, we turned our sights on another villain in our world: my father. We submitted our collected evidence to a private investigator in Salt Lake City. That PI did some major digging, and it turns out my father isn't quite the perfectionist he wants people to think he is. Apparently, he's really sloppy at covering his tracks. An inflated ego makes you careless. He must have just expected that nobody would be looking for trouble like this way out in the sticks of Wyoming.

"Wow. I can't believe it," I murmur, a smile on my lips.

There's so much good happening lately, it seems. So much to look forward to. I am finally starting to heal, and Ironside is, too. Soon, there's going to be a memorial for victims of Diesel's dark operation. It feels like closure must be right around the corner. But even if it isn't, I know I'll be okay. Ironside loves me, and I love him. We've already weathered such horrific storms together, and whatever happens, we'll get through it. Together.

"I love you," I tell him, grinning.

He leans in and kisses me softly, cupping my cheek. He pulls back and gazes at me with such adoration in his eyes. "I love you, too, Justine. To the moon and back."

"To the moon," I repeat in a murmur. I lean in to kiss him again.

But we're violently interrupted by a loud banging at the door. I cry out and duck down instinctively, while Ironside goes to grab his gun. "Stay down," he hisses at me as he cocks the gun and inches toward the door.

"Be careful!" I whisper back.

He gives me a nod, takes a deep breath, and opens the door. Immediately, I relax when I see that it's only Big Daddy. He raises an eyebrow at the gun pointed toward his heart and Ironside lets his shoulders slump, lowering the gun.

"Damn it, man. Don't surprise me like that," he groans.

Big Daddy doesn't say a word. There's a grim look on his face.

"What? What's wrong?" I ask, coming out from my hiding place to stand by Ironside at the door. Big Daddy remains wordless, but he lifts up an object for us to see.

To my confusion, it's a Heartbreaker kutte, only it's been badly damaged in a fire, and there's a fractured seam sewn right down the middle of the pierced heart.

"Shit," Ironside murmurs.

"What? What does it mean?" I ask.

Big Daddy looks at me and grunts, "It's a message."

"A message? Okay, then what does it say?" I question.

I look up at Ironside, and he looks dead serious.

"It's a declaration of war," he says.

~

Thank you so much for reading! I hope you enjoyed <3 If you have a moment, please leave a review. Other readers are dying to know what you thought.

I have plenty more bad boy romance for you, so make sure you check out my other books on the next couple of pages, and sign up for my newsletter to be notified when I have a new release on the way!

~Alexis Abbott

Trafficked

Stealing Her

The Assassin's Heart

Killing For Her

Abducted

KILLERS:

Hunter's Baby

I Hired A Hitman

STEPBROTHERS:

Ruthless

Criminal

GLITZ & GRIT:

Betting on Love

Vegas Boss

Rock Hard Bodyguard

Innocence For Sale: Jane

Redeeming Viktor

SEXY SEALs

Sweetheart for the SEAL

Sights on the SEAL

Romance:

Falling for her Boss (Novella)

Most Wanted: Lilly (Novella)

Bound as the World Burns (SFF)

<u>**Erotic Thriller:**</u>

THE DANGEROUS MEN SERIES:

The Narrow Path

Strayed from the Path

Path to Ruin

Alexis Abbott is a Wall Street Journal & USA Today bestselling author who writes about bad boys protecting their girls! Pick up her books today if you can't resist a bad boy who is a good man, and find yourself transported with super steamy sex, gritty suspense, and lots of romance.

She lives in beautiful St. John's, NL, Canada with her amazing husband.

facebook.com/abbottauthor

twitter.com/abbottauthor

instagram.com/alexisabbottauthor

bookbub.com/authors/alexis-abbott

pinterest.com/badboyromance

youtube.com/AlexisAbbott

ACKNOWLEDGMENTS

Thank you to my amazing Patrons. I'm constantly humbled and grateful for your support.

Ramona Cabrera
Melissa Hedrick
Virginia Swanson
Dawn Daughenbaugh
Don Doss
Stacie Currie

If you'd like to join them — and get my ebooks or paperbacks — you can find me here on Patreon.
https://www.patreon.com/alexisabbott

www.ingramcontent.com/pod-product-compliance
Lightning Source LLC
Chambersburg PA
CBHW021122190726
48288CB00008B/2448